SUPERSTITION
TRAIL

Other Books by L. W. Rogers

Brady's Revenge
The Twisted Trail

SUPERSTITION TRAIL

•

L. W. Rogers

AVALON BOOKS
NEW YORK

Published by Avalon Books,
an imprint of Thomas Bouregy & Co., Inc.
New York, NY

Library of Congress Cataloging-in-Publication Data

Rogers, L. W.
    Superstition trail / Loretta Rogers.
        p. cm.
    ISBN 978-0-8034-7620-2 (hardcover : acid-free paper)
I. Title.
    PS3618.O465S87 2011
    813'.6—dc23

                                        2011025795

PRINTED IN THE UNITED STATES OF AMERICA
ON ACID-FREE PAPER
BY RR DONNELLEY, HARRISONBURG, VIRGINIA

Chapter One

His side ached where the bullet had ripped through almost ten days ago. Gripping the saddle horn, Donovan cursed silently. He grunted against the pain as he lifted his foot to the stirrup. The effort sapped his strength and his legs buckled. He leaned heavily against the saddle and blinked at the darkness clouding his eyes.

"Mister?"

Donovan grunted again. He opened his eyes to pinlike slits to look at the barefoot youngster standing next to him. "Yeah, kid?"

"For a nickel, I can hold the horse while you haul yourself in the saddle."

Donovan fumbled in his vest pocket. "Don't seem to have a nickel." He flipped the boy a quarter. "Two bits do?"

"Yes, sir." The lad grinned as he caught the coin and dropped it into his overalls pocket.

Donovan drew in a deep breath. He gritted his teeth and set the toe of his boot in the stirrup. He felt the gelding shift sideways from the weight.

"General is a might headstrong when he takes it into his mind to be stubborn. Think you can hold him?"

The boy risked a glance up at Donovan. "I'm six, sir. Sure I can."

Donovan nodded.

The lad braced his feet and gripped the bridle's cheekstraps. "Hold still, horse. Can't you see your owner's hurt bad?"

1

Drawing on emotional toughness, Donovan swung into the saddle. His breath came in short gasps as he gathered the reins.

"Mister?"

"Yeah?"

"You're bleedin'. My ma can fix you right up."

"Don't need fixin', boy. Need to get on my way."

The youngster pulled a bandanna from his back pocket and handed it up to Donovan. "Here. You need this more'n me."

Taking the cloth, Donovan wadded it into a ball and tucked it inside his shirt against the bullet hole. When he adjusted his weight in the saddle, his side rebelled.

"Donovan?"

Ignoring the terseness in the sheriff's voice, Donovan squinted against the sun's rays. "You can let go the reins now, boy. 'Preciate your help." He turned the gray gelding toward the raspy voice. "Something on your mind, Sheriff?"

"Man can get himself a bad case of dead if he don't allow time to heal." Sheriff Tom Horn nodded toward the bloodied spot on Donovan's shirt.

"Got me a ranch to claim, Sheriff."

"One thing you oughta know."

"You gonna stand there and talk me to death?"

Tom Horn bunched his eyebrows. "Rumor has it, Slaughter bought himself a mail-order bride not so long ago. If'n I was you, I'd ride in easylike. Don't make no never mind that Jack Slaughter was a womanizing double-dealing snake. And it don't matter that he tried to backshoot you to get the deed to his ranch back. His missus might not take kindly to you makin' her a widow."

Donovan bristled. "Poker game was fair and square. Witnesses said so."

The sheriff scratched his whiskered jaw. "No call to get riled. I'm just saying that sometimes folks don't get the right of things in the telling. Slaughter associated himself with some bad hombres. His missus probably won't know that either."

"How far to the Circle S?"

"Look, Donovan, you're new to these parts. Slaughter was into some bad stuff. Couldn't never prove it though. My advice to you is to forget about claiming the Circle S and ride on back to where you belong."

"How far, Sheriff?" Donovan knew if he didn't get moving soon that he might fall out of the saddle. As gunshot wounds went, this wasn't the worst he'd experienced. He'd heal, but he refused do it in a flea-bitten hotel or bunking in a stall at the livery stable.

"You're one stubborn cuss." The sheriff pointed toward a range of mountains. "As the crow flies, thirty miles. By horseback, add another twenty. You can shave off about ten if you cut across Superstition Mountain. That is . . . if you don't bleed to death first."

Donovan nodded. "I'll live. Much obliged for squaring things with the judge."

"Pure and simple case of self-defense." The sheriff's voice was matter-of-fact.

"Keep the sun to your back, Sheriff."

Donovan gripped the saddle horn to keep from swaying. Speaking softly to the gelding, he nudged it toward the snow-capped mountains. By nightfall he'd covered ten bone-jarring miles.

He hadn't realized he'd fallen asleep in the saddle until the sound of splashing awakened him. He became aware that the gelding stood at the edge of a stream and had pawed at the water before drinking. Exhaustion tugged at Donovan as he slid from the horse's back.

Gathering his strength, he loosened the cinch but left the saddle in place, knowing the effort it would take to lift it. After hobbling the horse, Donovan collected twigs and small branches and banked a fire. When the coffeepot was set, he stripped off his shirt and walked to the stream's edge. He used the waning light to cleanse the wound. Then, rinsing blood from the bandanna, he held it against the fevered area while rummaging in his saddlebag for a clean shirt and a bottle of rye.

Gritting his teeth against the burn, he poured a liberal amount of alcohol over the wound. He bunched the bandanna against the red, puckered area, buttoned the shirt, then laced a cup of coffee with whiskey. He settled against a tree to let exhaustion overtake him.

He drifted in and out of sleep, his conscious moments plagued by nightmares. Time had left its scars on him. Faces of lifeless settlers plagued his slumber. He'd lain wounded and left for dead while his father and brother were hanged by night riders—the house and barn torched, the livestock driven off.

He'd lived, nursed his wounds, and drifted from town to town, ranch to ranch, saloon to saloon. He'd learned cunning and how to play poker, reading the quirks of the other players. And he'd drifted, always searching for faces. He needed vengeance. He needed to uphold the vow he'd made—to find the men who had stolen his livestock, stolen his land, and murdered his family.

Jack Slaughter hadn't recognized the kid he planted three slugs into—a kid of seventeen, now a man just past thirty. Donovan remembered . . . remembered the hawked nose, the eyes lit with a crazy meanness, and the reddish stubble covering his face.

Five men had been found and punished; one remained. A man's face hidden in the night's dark shadows—a man with a phlegmy voice and a penchant for spitting on his victims.

Donovan surrendered to his nightmares.
He slept.

Soft nickers awakened Donovan. He pried an eye open. Rays filtering through the tree branches caused him to shut it again. When he moved slightly, his side protested. The inside of his mouth felt like dry cotton. He was no longer propped against the tree, but lay on his side covered with a blanket. The rich aroma of coffee tantalized his nostrils.

How long had he been here like this, unable to move? And where was he? He searched his mind thoroughly. Then, with great care, he turned his head and slanted his eyes toward the back of the man squatting at the fire.

Memories flooded in then, and it all came back to him. He'd ridden into Blountstown looking for a hot bath, a thick steak, and a poker game. He recalled the wound in his side; he'd been backshot by a sidewinder named Jack Slaughter.

Donovan felt weakness overcoming him. He didn't like the feeling. It brought back too many memories of another time when he'd been laid up. He shifted his focus back to the man who now approached him with a cup of coffee in one hand and a plate of food in the other.

"Figured you'd be wakin' pretty soon. Reckon you could do with a bite of food."

Donovan scooted upright against the tree. Wrapping his hands around the cup of coffee, he worked to clear his dry throat. "I'm obliged." He spoke so weakly he barely recognized his own voice. "You got a name?"

"Bert Nolan." The man set the plate of food next to Donovan, then ambled back to the fire.

After filling his cup with coffee and a plate with beans and bacon, Nolan settled against his saddle and stretched his long legs.

To anyone else it might appear that Bert Nolan was as re-laxed as a mud turtle sunning itself on a log. Donovan knew better. He hadn't missed the low-lidded covert glances.

He choked on the first sip of coffee.

"Go easy, friend. You've been unconscious for three days."

Donovan blew to cool the steaming liquid and sipped again. Setting the cup aside, he lifted the plate and wolfed down the meal. When he was sated, he finished off the coffee and held out the cup for more. "Most drifters would've stolen my horse, gear, and weapons, and probably my boots and money. What makes you a do-gooder?" Donovan closed his eyes and heaved a sigh. Being awake and talking had sapped his energy.

The man pulled back his leather vest to reveal a badge. "I'm a deputy marshal out of Apache Junction." His laugh sounded more like a snort to Donovan. "First time anybody's called me a do-gooder." The deputy chuckled again, then lifted his own cup of coffee to take a sip. "And just for the record, I did go through your gear. Finding a man more dead than alive with a festerin' bullet hole in his side sorta tickles my curiosity."

"I reckon you found the paper from Sheriff Horn signed by the judge?"

"Yup." Deputy Bert Nolan refilled both their cups. "You're fair and square with the law."

"Where you headed, Deputy?"

Nolan pointed toward the northwest. "Folks been reporting some funny goings-on in the Superstition Mountains."

"How so?"

"Oh, things like a woman screaming. Strange red lights bobbing up and down." The deputy scratched under his armpit. "Those are things that are probably easily explained. It's the disappearance of herds of cattle and the drovers that concerns me."

Donovan sat forward. "How can a herd of a thousand or more steers disappear without a trace?"

"I'm mostly thinking it's the imagination of some poor prospector whose addlepated from too much sun and maybe too much mescal."

Donovan harrumphed. "How do you explain the screaming woman?"

"Can't. Lots of Indian legends about the Superstition Mountains. I figure that the screamin' folks claim to hear is nothing more than the wind blowing up through a hole in one of the canyons." Nolan gathered up the plates and cups. He spoke over his shoulder as he ambled toward the stream. "Either way, it's my job to check it out."

"Mind some company? I'm riding that way myself." Part Comanche is what Donovan was, according to all accounts he'd ever heard or seen. That and Irish from his long-dead pa. It wasn't his nature to tend another man's business—especially when a man preferred riding alone. And as for the "funny goings-on," Donovan didn't scare easily.

Deputy Nolan handed him a canteen. "I'm due back in Apache Junction next week. Seeing as how I couldn't leave you to the buzzards, me an' my ole pony got to put some miles behind us."

The deputy hefted the saddle from the ground. "If'n I were you, I'd rest a few more days. Break open that wound again, and you might not live to see the next sunrise."

Twenty minutes later, shortly before noon, Donovan sat propped against the tree and watched Deputy Marshal Bert Nolan ride out of sight.

Chapter Two

In mid-July, Donovan skylined himself on a spiny ridgetop in the Superstition Mountains. The weeks of travel had hidden the ravages of pain beneath a coating of trail dust.

The land lay golden beneath the sun's burning pool. Clouds, rambunctious in the western wind, billowed over the farthermost rim of the mountains, patching the land with drifting shadows. A breeze gushed upward out of the valley, washing the rim in a cooling surge of energy.

He sat on the back of his horse with his hands resting on the pommel of the saddle. The gelding pawed the earth, and Donovan reached forward to pat the animal's neck.

He took one last look at the land lying wide and handsome in every direction, beckoning and challenging Donovan to claim it as his own.

He squinted up at the already fierce sun, and then, shading his eyes, turned his attention to the sky. A flock of birds flitted and swayed on the airy rushes of the valley.

"Buzzards." Donovan spoke only to the gelding. "They've come to feed on something." He shrugged off fleeting thoughts of deputy marshal Bert Nolan.

He nudged his boot heels against the flanks of his mount and guided the gray gelding onto the trail leading down from the ridge. His attention was riveted to the descent, so much so that he failed to notice a diaphanous tendril of smoke rising from an unseen campfire, a wilderness warning for the watchful to beware.

* * *

8

Reaching the floor of the valley, he rode toward the creek. Within sight of water, a covey of quail broke from cover, spooking the gelding. Donovan kept a tight grip on the reins, bringing the startled horse under control.

Only a scar remained where the bullet hole in Donovan's side had healed. There were days when he felt no residual effects, but when the horse crow-hopped, nearly toppling Donovan from the saddle, pain, hot and searing, caused perspiration to pop out on his brow.

After settling the animal, he pressed his hand against the ache. He drew oxygen into his lungs, held it, and then slowly breathed out. He shifted his weight to ease his punished side.

When the horse stamped its impatience, Donovan said, "Easy does it, big fellow. If my calculations are right, we've been on Slaughter land for at least an hour."

The horse grunted and flicked its ears as if listening to the man on his back.

"Yeah, I hear you, friend. I'm ready for a good meal and a soft bed to rest my weary bones too." Donovan chuckled when the gelding tossed its head up and down and squealed.

It'd been a week since Donovan had burned his tongue on a cup of good strong coffee, the last of his supply, and his beans and bacon had run out two days ago.

Drawing in a breath, he nudged the gelding forward. "C'mon, General. Time's a'wastin'."

The sun burned high when he sniffed the summer air and discovered the scent of roasting meat and the unmistakable aroma of coffee. He stopped and peered through levels of light and shade, of gloom and slanted sunlight, and at last he caught sight of the ranch house and then the barn.

The lack of activity in the yard and around the outbuildings disturbed him. By no means was it a large operation. Donovan figured a ranch the size of the Circle S could support a half dozen or more hands.

Caution tugged at him. He chided himself when tension prickled his spine. No one expected his arrival. And fifty miles from Blountstown, there was no one to connect him to the death of Jack Slaughter.

Donovan splashed across the creek, making enough noise to announce his approach.

Chapter Three

The Slaughter Ranch lay silent beneath the noonday sun. From time to time a few thin, scudding clouds drifted across the sky. Nothing moved in the corrals or in the open spaces between the outbuildings. Save for the whisper of a warm, dry breeze and an occasional whinny from the barn, there was no sound.

Dulcie Slaughter stood just inside the barn door, hidden in the shadows. She lifted a hand to shade her eyes from the sun's glare while she watched the lone rider guide his horse down the steep pitch of the mountain and then splash across Mossy Creek.

He sat tall in the saddle, his movements fluid with the stocky dapple-gray beneath him.

She watched him slow the horse when he topped the rise and looked toward where the ranch house stood. When he rode to the center of the yard, she reached for the rifle propped against the barn wall. Still she stayed to the shadows.

"Hello, the house." Donovan's deep voice shattered the silence. "Anyone about?"

Dulcie levered a cartridge into the rifle's chamber and watched the man tense at the sound of the click. "State your business, mister."

When he rose to dismount, she warned, "Don't recall inviting you to step down. Hands where I can see them."

He settled back into the saddle. "This the Slaughter Ranch?"

"Depends on who's asking."

From where she stood, Dulcie knew she had the advantage. Though his eyes looked toward the sound of her voice, the shadows hid her.

Donovan squinted against the flash of light that bounced off the rifle's barrel. When Sheriff Horn mentioned Slaughter had bought himself a mail-order bride, Donovan had envisioned a simpering female from back East—certainly not a woman with enough sand in her backbone to stand her ground against a stranger.

He decided now wasn't the time to shove the signed deed under her nose that claimed the Circle S as his.

Dulcie stepped from the barn. Heart pounding, she stood with her feet apart, the Winchester braced against her shoulder.

Donovan obeyed her command and lifted his hands. "If this is the Slaughter Ranch, I heard the owner was hiring."

"You have a name?"

"Yes, ma'am. Donovan."

"Can you prove it?"

"Look, lady, my arms are getting mighty tired, and I don't take kindly to sitting in the hot sun staring down at the business end of a rifle."

Dulcie kept the weapon trained at his heart. "This is the Slaughter Ranch. I am the owner, and how do I know you're who you say you are?"

"Reckon you'll have to take my word for it, ma'am. I'm not wanted by the law, and my only business is needin' a job that pays a fair wage."

Relief swept over her when a voice from the porch called out, "I got 'im covered, Miz Dulcie. You kin rest easy now."

"Thanks, Teaspoon." She offered a brief smile toward a grizzled old cowboy who stood on the top step with a Winchester double-barrel trained at Donovan. "What do you think, Teaspoon?"

The old ranch hand lowered his shotgun. "Don't look like no outlaw. 'Sides, if'n he was up to no good, he wouldn'a rode in boldlike, smack-dab in the middle o' the day." The old man spat a string of brown tobacco juice across the yard. He dragged the sleeve of his checkered shirt across his mouth. "Your call, Miz Dulcie. Either way, cowhand or drifter, we shorely need help roundin' up the stock."

"All right, Teaspoon. I trust your judgment." She too lowered her rifle. "Step down, Mr. Donovan. Settle your horse inside the corral. After you stow your gear in the bunkhouse, join us for lunch."

Donovan was a man of large growth, but it was a trim-boned bigness. Tall, much taller than ordinary, and long of legs and arms, he was a powerfully built man, strong and broad.

His features were bold and hinted of humor and wry observation. In contrast to his dark looks, his eyes were as blue as the depths of a frozen pond and as impossible to fathom. She thought they were the eyes of a man accustomed to hiding his inner feelings.

Donovan led the gelding to the corral. He loosened the girth and slid the saddle from the animal's sweaty back. Then, after removing the bridle, he placed a firm slap on the gray's neck. He watched as the horse lay down, rolled, and then stood again to shake dust from its body.

Donovan spoke to the animal, promising a good rubdown and an extra ration of oats. He hefted the gear and strode to the bunkhouse. He'd stow his gear later. Right now he intended to wash off a week's layer of dust and put on a clean shirt.

Balancing the saddle and bridle on the bunkhouse porch railing, he lifted the latch and shoved open the door. He half-expected to see a few ranch hands lolling on their bunks. He blinked to adjust his eyes to the dim interior.

No shirts hung from wall knobs, no boots beneath bunks, no empty whiskey bottles or coffee cups lining the scarred wooden table in the center of the room. Only cobwebs and the fading odor of hardworking men greeted him.

"Easy there, young feller. Didn't mean to spook ya." Donovan willed himself not to go into a crouch and reach for the .45 on his hip when the aged wrangler eased up behind him.

For a moment the two men eyed each other as if sizing up the other's mettle. Teaspoon Griffin broke the silence. "Take yer pick, sonny. 'Ceptin' for that one by the stove, ain't nobody gonna fight you for neither an upper or lower bunk."

"The ranch in trouble . . . financially?" Donovan tossed his rucksack on a lower bunk tucked in a corner and away from the door.

The old cowboy said, "Ain't my business to say." He peered around as if checking to see if anyone was listening. "I can tell ya this, Miz Dulcie needs all the help she can get. Since some jackleg's done gone and kilt her husband, and I ain't saying he didn't deserve it, well, the men just up and quit, and—"

The melodic voice calling from across the yard stilled the old man. He scratched beneath his scruff of whiskers. "Sometimes I flap my jaws too much. C'mon, food's gettin' cold."

Donovan ambled across the yard behind Teaspoon Griffin. He eyed the woman standing on the porch. One long braid draped over her shoulder. Her hair reminded him of summer wheat.

She appeared not much younger than himself. There was a lushness about her—pretty, perhaps beautiful, with large brown eyes and a milkmaid's complexion. But such attractiveness, he knew only too well, would not last forever. The sun was the mortal enemy of women who endured the rigors of ranch life.

A willow of a girl, he thought, and then reminded himself that he'd made her a widow.

With a slight grunt, Dulcie used both hands to set the heavy Dutch oven filled with beef stew on the table. She walked back to the stove to pull a pan of hot biscuits from the oven.

She looked around the room. This wasn't what she'd imagined when she'd answered the ad in the *New York Sentinel* to come to this isolated ranch in Gold Canyon, halfway between here and nowhere. Far from it. The ad she'd read sounded as romantic as the man who had placed it. She had accepted the fare he'd sent for travel, gathered her meager belongings, and without looking back, had set out on this journey to what she intended would be a new beginning.

Now here she was stuck in the middle of the boondocks and the widow of a man whose eyes had sometimes frightened her. Shaking her head at the thought, she absently brushed a wrinkle from the checkered tablecloth. She was about to reach for the coffeepot when the door opened.

Donovan's muscular frame filled the doorway. A sudden tension filled her, and she wondered if he felt it too. She sensed there was nothing that would frighten this man. That he was a man who knew himself, knew his strengths and his weaknesses, who measured himself by the hard land and the men who lived in it.

There had been other men who visited the ranch when her husband was alive. Some of them frightened her, but none of them had ever disturbed her like Donovan did.

She started to speak but didn't trust her voice. She drew back a little and smoothed her apron. "Sit before the food gets cold."

Donovan accepted another cup of coffee. He savored the richness of the stew as he sopped a hot biscuit in the pool of thick broth on his plate. "Best meal I've eaten in a long while, ma'am. Trail food gets mighty tiresome."

"Please, I prefer Mrs. Slaughter to ma'am."

"Yes, ma'am . . . er . . . Mrs. Slaughter. Just so you know, there's no Mister in front of my name."

She offered a smile. "All right, Donovan. Let's get down to business. Are you handy with a gun?"

He liked this slip of a woman. She looked a man square in the eye when she talked and didn't bandy around words. "I can hold my own when need be."

"Good. You're hired. Fifteen dollars a month, all the food you can eat, and a bonus when we get my cattle to market."

"Beg pardon, Mrs. Slaughter, but what about your husband? Might he want a say in this?" Donovan cut his eyes toward the old cowboy seated across the table.

"Ain't no never mind of your'n 'bout the decisions Miz Dulcie makes."

Dulcie reached across the table and gently patted the man's arm. "It's all right, Teaspoon."

Donovan thought he saw her shudder. Whatever he saw, the moment was fleeting.

"I'm a widow, Donovan. A month ago, my husband rode to Blountstown to hire extra men to help with the cattle drive. He was murdered." Her voice was soft and broken.

The chill spidering up Donovan's spine clashed with the flush under his bandanna. Murdered? He wondered how much she knew about her husband's death.

"Did the sheriff bring you the news?"

"No. One of the hands from Mr. Humphrey's ranch, the Rocking H, brought my husband's body home. He said a drifter had accused Jack of cheating at cards and, without provocation, shot my husband." Dulcie dabbed the tears from her eyes.

"Did this ranch hand from the Rocking H know the feller who shot your husband?"

The fine meal in Donovan's stomach now sat like rocks. He laid the biscuit aside and rested his wrists against the table's edge, expectant of her answer.

"Only that the man who shot my husband was a double-dealing skunk of a cardsharp named Ace."

"Any description of this . . . Ace?"

"None, but I hope whoever he is rots in hell."

Her words stung. Donovan stood. "I realize this is an emotional time for you." He bowed slightly. "If you'll excuse me, my horse needs tending."

She stood as if taking full stock of him. "Don't go just yet, Donovan. Since my husband's death, strange things are happening." She paced back and forth.

"Yep," Teaspoon chimed in. "First, all the men quit. Said they weren't takin' no orders from a woman boss, 'specially one from the East."

Dulcie blinked back tears. She poured each of them another cup of coffee and took a seat, inviting Donovan to join her again. "It isn't that, as much as the strange dancing lights up in the mountains. And those horrible screams, like someone torturing a woman." She shuddered and wrapped her arms about her. "And when Teaspoon and I rode out to check on the livestock, we found dead cattle around one of the watering holes."

"Poisoned?" Donovan asked.

She nodded. Her voice was quiet. "That isn't all. A few nights ago, about midnight, men rode through the yard, shooting."

In his own way, Donovan felt deeply for her troubles. "Get a look at them?"

"No. They were dressed in black and rode dark horses. They blended with the night." She folded her arms across her chest. "I must get my cattle to market, Donovan. My husband left me little money. This ranch is my only asset."

Relief settled over Donovan, and his spirits rose a little.

"You could go back East. Ranch life, especially a ranch as remote as this, is no place for a woman alone."

"There's nothing for me in New York. No family, nothing. Everything I have is here, and I refuse to be frightened off my land."

Donovan's gut feelings told him that someone was capitalizing on Jack Slaughter's death. But who? "Mrs. Slaughter, got any ideas who would want to frighten you enough to leave?"

She shrugged. "Frighten me off? Why . . . I don't know. It's a small ranch. We barely run six hundred head of cattle. I'm no competition for any of the larger ranchers."

Donovan didn't miss the struggle in Dulcie's voice, nor the way she worried her bottom lip. He got to his feet, standing tall and straight. Now certainly wasn't the time to tell her that she no longer owned the Circle S. He felt lower than a snake's belly.

"What have you done about hiring men, Mrs. Slaughter?"

She breathed out a long sigh. "Teaspoon rode over to the Rocking H to see if Mr. Humphrey would lend us a few men. He said with his own drive under way that he could barely spare three. But he'd send Hank, Mayo, and Sims over tomorrow."

"Why didn't you ask him to join your herd with his?" Donovan rocked the chair back on its legs.

Her mouth formed a surprised O. She seemed puzzled. "Teaspoon, did you ask?"

The old cowhand concentrated on the toe of his boot. "Yes'm. Didn't want to upset you. The percentage Humphrey wanted off the top of what your stock brought at market wouldn've left hardly enough to buy winter feed, let alone hire a new crew and pay wages."

Dulcie huffed out a snort. "Then Clive Humphrey can eat my dust. I'll get my few hundred head of cows to market before he can push his two thousand cows across to . . . to wherever he's herding them."

"Steers, Miz Dulcie. They're steers."

She stamped her foot. "Cows, steers . . . what difference does it make what they're called?" Her brows furrowed. "Donovan, how soon can we start roundup?"

It was obvious Dulcie Slaughter knew little about herding cattle. "Six hundred beeves and four men droving . . . lot of work, ma'am."

"Six." She placed her hands on her hips. "I'll drive the cook wagon. That will free Teaspoon to help with the herd."

"Oh, but Miz Dulcie," the old cowboy protested, "a cattle drive ain't no place for a citified lady."

She held up her hand. "No arguments. I'm going." She turned to Donovan. "Donovan, is there a way to beat Mr. Humphrey and get my herd to market first?"

He studied her for a long moment. Every cattleman knew bringing a woman on a cattle drive was bad luck. Still, he was a gambler, and he'd bet this woman played by her own rules and made her own luck.

Chapter Four

A little after midnight, an owl hooted and was answered with a returning call signaling an all clear in the camp. Two horsemen rode into the firelight. Neither waited for an invitation to dismount.

Two men who had been squatting next to the fire stood. The second one rubbed his face, filling the silence with a raw, scratchy sound. "'Bout time the boss sent us some relief. I'm tired of sleeping on the cold, hard ground. And Dink here cain't cook worth spit. 'Sides, I don't like campin' on Indian burial grounds."

"What's the matter, Vesper? You believe in spooks, do you?"

"Hell, Mayo. There's more'n just me and Dink up here on this mountain. Sure, it's us what's ridin' up and down flashing pot lights in every which direction"—Vesper grabbed the reins of his horse and swung into the saddle—"but this is Apache land, and . . ."

The pock-faced man named Mayo said, "Ain't no more Apaches in these mountains. Only ones around are miles away on the reservation. And everybody knows that Chief Three Feathers and his people are too old and tired to fight any more battles."

"Don't make no never mind," Vesper said. "This place gives me the willies." He looked at his companion. "You coming, Dink?" Vesper sat on his horse impatiently and watched while the two relief gunmen settled by the fire.

Mayo said, "Humphrey wants you to pay Miz Slaughter a surprise visit. Like maybe this time set fire to her barn."

Dink sniggered. "Mebbe me and Vesper'll do more'n set fire to the barn. Mebbe we'll pay a special call on that pretty little widder lady."

In one swift motion Mayo stood, reached up, and grabbed the cowboy's shirt, nearly hauling him out of the saddle. "Humphrey'll peel your hide if you go messing with the woman. He's got his own eyes set on her."

He twisted the shirt with his beefy fist until Dink choked out a gasp. "Okay . . . ain't no call to get sore."

Mayo sneered. "You've been warned. Now get on down the mountain and do what you're paid to do. Scare the woman and that old cowhand of hers so bad the starch will slide right out of their backbones."

Donovan lay with his hands behind his head. He gritted his teeth. Listening to the thunderous snores that filled the room, he wondered when Teaspoon Griffin would finally settle into an easy slumber.

He rolled off the bunk and padded in his stocking feet to open the bunkhouse door. Stepping onto the porch, he breathed in the warm night air.

The moon, as bright as a shiny silver dollar, was balanced neatly on the rim of the canyon. Donovan peered through the darkness at the hills, a slow, studying gaze. Not spotting anything out of the ordinary, he reasoned perhaps the mysterious glowing that folks reported seeing was the northern lights. The Indians called it the Dance of the Spirits. He'd never seen the illuminations himself and didn't put much stock in legends.

He glanced over at the main house. It was dark. Nothing seemed out of the ordinary. No strange lights, no mysterious screaming woman.

For some inexplicable reason, he had a feeling that all wasn't as it seemed, that trouble was out there, waiting. It hung in the night air like something tangible.

With a resigned shrug he walked back inside, stretched out on the bunk, and closed his eyes.

Donovan didn't know what had stirred him from bone-tired sleep. The shrill whinny of a horse jerked him awake. Listening intently, Donovan rolled off the bunk, reached for his gunbelt, and strapped it around his waist. After another tremulous whinny, he heard the rattle and snap of stirrups and the clamber of hooves.

Without bothering to pull on his boots, in two long strides he crossed the bunkhouse floor to where Teaspoon Griffin slept. Donovan shook the old man's shoulder until he came wide-awake.

"Tarnation," Teaspoon's voice rasped. "It's the middle of the night. Whadda you want?"

"Grab your pistol. Something's spooking my horse."

Teaspoon raised up, bracing himself on one elbow. "Gawldang rhemytism. Takes a minute to work the kinks outta these ol' joints of mine." He coughed and scrubbed his eyes with the heels of his hands. "Gimme my double barrel. Ain't so good with a handgun no more."

Donovan impatiently waited for the old man to roll off the bunk, reach down for the suspenders at his hips, and pull the straps over his shoulders. He shoved the shotgun toward the old man. "Stay low."

With revolver in hand, Donovan strode across the room to peer out the small window. He watched the gelding rear up with wild exuberance, snorting and pawing as he bucked and raced around the corral.

"What is it, Donovan? Whadda you see out there?"

A scream from the main house knotted the muscles between Donovan's shoulder blades. Unable to hold himself back any longer, he jerked open the bunkhouse door and eased outside as he crouched low, his Colt Peacemaker gripped tight, and made his way to the end of the porch. He dashed across the yard toward the house.

A rider brandishing a torch raced from behind one of the barns. Donovan aimed and fired. The Colt Peacemaker bucked in his hand.

Dropping the torch, the rider yowled and lurched forward in the saddle. A second rider rode across the yard, ramming his horse against Donovan and knocking him to the ground. His heart pulsed wildly as he rolled away from the hooves.

A shotgun blast shattered the night.

Coming to his knees, Donovan glanced over his shoulder to see who had fired. Teaspoon was panting, his bone-white face revealing the awful effort it took for him to hustle across the yard.

Donovan swung his revolver up. Red flame burst from the barrel as he pulled the trigger. The bullet missed its mark as the night riders disappeared into the darkness.

Donovan rotated on his knees at Dulcie's shrill cry. "The barn! They've set the barn on fire."

The frightened screams of horses and a cow's bawling drew Dulcie to the structure already engulfed in flames. Donovan sprinted after her. He caught her by the arms. "We need wet blankets, anything to put over the animals' eyes."

"I-I don't understand." The red glow from the blaze revealed the fright on her face.

Donovan clipped off his explanation. "Horses are afraid of fire. They'll burn to death before running through the flames. I need to cover their heads with anything wet."

He watched Dulcie lift the hem of her nightgown, and without hesitation or question, she dashed toward the house. He turned to Teaspoon. "Get a bucket of water and soak me down good." Donovan pulled the bandanna from his back pocket and tied it over his mouth and nose.

"Better if'n you dunk yourself in the horse trough. You'll

be wetter than a drowned turkey before I kin prime the pump and fill a bucket."

Donovan nodded his understanding and sprinted toward the corral. In one hurdle, he cleared the top post. By the time he hauled his sopping wet body from the horse trough, Dulcie was racing toward him with an armload of dripping tablecloths. He noticed she had hastily changed from her nightgown to a dress and had pulled the skirt up between her legs, tucking the hem into the waistband to form a pair of bloomers.

"Where the hell you think you're going?"

"They're my animals, Donovan. My mare is in there and so is the milk cow and two baby calves, and Wheeler, my husband's gelding."

"No time to argue about stubborn foolishness." He pointed toward the horse trough. "Go soak yourself."

"What?"

"Don't stand there with your mouth gaped open, woman! Drench yourself good to keep from catching on fire."

Unable to hold himself back any longer, Donovan gathered the wet tablecloths to his chest and rushed through the smoke-filled barn door.

He knew by the squeals and erratic movements the animals were frantic. Fumes seared his lungs. He squinted through the smoke until he located the mare. He tossed a wet cloth over the pinto's head, then, swinging the stall door wide, grabbed the halter's cheekstrap and tugged. The horse reared. Donovan held tight. He spoke to the animal. "Easy does it, girl. Work with me here." He rubbed his hand down her neck, crooning to her, and then, using the strength in his powerful arms, led the mare out of the stall and down the aisle. The frightened animal reared again, nearly jerking Donovan's arm from its socket.

In the gray haze, he spotted a quirt hanging from a nail on a post. He snatched it, gripping the handle. He gagged on the smoke. Fire licked at the water-thirsty beams. His eyes smarted, and he blinked against the tears.

Dulcie called his name. "Donovan?"

"Over here . . . get the calves."

Dulcie pushed past him.

The mare whinnied in terror. "Easy, girl . . . easy. You'll be safe in minute." Donovan let go of the halter. He drew back his arm and brought the quirt down across the mare's rump. As soon as the startled animal bolted through the flames and out the barn door, Donovan called out, "You okay, Mrs. Slaughter?"

"Yes. Please, just get the milk cow and my husband's horse out of there."

Donovan followed the sound of her voice and saw that she had draped wet clothes over the calves' heads.

She struggled to lift the smallest into her arms. "The chickens, oh please, the chickens. We must save them."

"Forget the chickens and get yourself out. Those beams aren't going to hold much longer." Donovan grabbed one of the calves up into his arms and sprinted toward the door. Dulcie followed close on his heels.

Teaspoon stood at the doorway with a bucket in his hand. The moment Donovan came out, gasping for air, the old cowboy let water fly, soaking Donovan.

Donovan sucked air into his lungs. Before he plowed back into the barn, he said, "See to Mrs. Slaughter and the animals."

With his hands stretched in front of him, Donovan groped his way through the thick smoke, using the sound of the gelding's screams to guide him.

Inside the barn's last stall, the panicked buckskin kicked at the rear wall. Donovan lifted his arm to shield his eyes from the smoke. He coughed to clear his lungs. He dodged a burning beam that crashed in front of him.

He looked over his shoulder. The entire barn was ablaze. A wall of flames blocked both escape routes. He squinted, searching through the smoky haze until he spotted a shovel.

Knowing the danger of being kicked to death by the panicked gelding, Donovan opened the stall door and edged in. He used his shoulder to push the horse aside. Then, sliding the shovel between the back wall planks, he pried and kicked until he had an opening large enough to squeeze his body through.

He yelled, "Teaspoon . . . on the double . . . here!"

As soon as he saw the old wrangler huffing around the barn with Dulcie close on his heels, Donovan said, "Help me pull the boards off. It's the only way to get the gelding out."

Working as a unit, they removed four boards. Donovan reached in and grabbed the horse by the tail and tugged. The frightened animal backed out, nearly bowling Teaspoon over, and then raced toward the corral. It squealed and grunted as if seeking comfort from Donovan's gelding and the pinto mare.

In the next instant, Donovan was hit in the face by a flurry of feathers. Three hens and a rooster made their escape from the fiery inferno.

Pitiful mewlings caused Dulcie to cry out. "The kittens! I forgot about them." She looked up at Donovan, her eyes pleading.

"Confound it, woman, how many more animals are in there?" He snorted his aggravation.

"Never mind. I'll get them myself."

Donovan grabbed her around the waist and swung her into Teaspoon's arms. Before he could suck in a breath and enter the crumbling structure, three kittens—one yellow tabby and two calicoes—raced through the opening. Donovan snatched the remaining tablecloth from Dulcie's hands and tossed it over the kittens while Dulcie stooped down and bundled the mewling babies into her arms.

She looked up. "You're a good man, Donovan. Thank you."

Standing there, holding the kittens, Dulcie Slaughter reminded him of a lost waif.

"I'm afraid the barn's a total loss, Mrs. Slaughter. At least the fire didn't jump to the second barn or to the house." An unexpected spasm of coughs wracked Donovan's chest.

Still cradling the kittens in her arms, Dulcie said, "Teaspoon, you and Donovan come to the house. I'll make coffee."

"Might you put a little red-eye in it to knock back the smoke from our guzzles, Miz Dulcie?"

"You know I don't hold with drinking." A weary smile teased her lips. "This time is an exception."

Donovan's voice was quiet. The tone reflected the seriousness of his question. "Mrs. Slaughter, who would want you out bad enough to set your barn on fire?"

Chapter Five

Tell me about your husband, Mrs. Slaughter." Donovan glanced up as she filled his cup.

"There isn't much I know." She set the coffeepot in the center of the table. "Jack and I were only married five months when he was killed."

Donovan paused in the turning of his cup on the table. He waited for her to continue. He found himself liking the stillness of her face. It was the shadowing around her eyes that disturbed him.

"He, that is, Jack, said he was an orphan. His parents died in a wagon train massacre when he was fifteen. He knocked around working odd jobs, living from hand to mouth, when the man who owned this ranch took him in. Having no heirs when Mr. Singer passed on, he willed the ranch to my husband."

"Handy."

It made no sense, a woman living like this. Not this woman anyway. He didn't consider himself an expert on women, but he knew the difference between saloon gals and refined ladies. And in his estimation, Dulcie Slaughter had all the markings of someone raised with culture.

She looked at him, not understanding his use of the word, and she said as much. " 'Handy'? I'm afraid I don't understand."

"Singer . . . Slaughter . . . Circle S. That's what I mean. Handy."

"Life is filled with coincidences, Donovan."

"You believe that, Mrs. Slaughter?" Had Jack Slaughter murdered Singer? Donovan wanted to crush the cup in his hands. He blinked back the visions of Slaughter tightening the nooses around his father's and brother's necks. Her words brought him back to reality.

"Yes, I do."

He studied her for a minute, and she met his eyes without flinching, a little puzzled and faintly bemused.

"Interesting," he said.

He glanced across the table at the old cowhand who'd held his peace. Teaspoon winked at Donovan as if to say he understood. He reached for the whiskey bottle and added a tipple to his cup. "For my rhemytism." He shoved back the chair. "I'm takin' my weary bones back to bed."

"Think the men from the Rocking H will show tomorrow, Teaspoon?" asked Donovan.

"'Spect so."

"Good. Soon as they ride in, we'll start gathering the cattle and horses for the remuda."

"Me too, Donovan."

"No, ma'am. Your job is to stock the chuck wagon with as many supplies as you have on hand and whatever female necessities you need for your own comfort."

This time he read excitement in her eyes. When he rose to leave, she said, "Why did you ask about my husband?"

"Wondered what kind of man he was . . . did he have shady dealings with anyone—"

She held up her hand, her voice stern. "Enough! I didn't know my husband very well, but I'll brook no one castigating his good name. At least until proven otherwise."

Castigate wasn't a word Donovan knew. It did prove what he suspected—Dulcie Slaughter was no ordinary woman.

"My apologies, Mrs. Slaughter." At the door and with a

backward glance, he said, "If your husband didn't have enemies, then there's another reason why someone is trying to
scare you off this place."

Dulcie peered up at him, then continued clearing the table.
"Well, a few days after my husband's death, Mr. Humphrey rode
over to pay his condolences, and . . . he offered to buy the ranch
for a generous amount." Quiet for a long moment, finally she
blinked.

"Having second thoughts about saying no?"

Dulcie's brown eyes clashed with eyes the color of a cloudy
sky. "Your business, Donovan, is getting my herd to market.
Nothing more."

She turned on her heel, without so much as a parting word,
and walked away.

Dulcie placed her hand over the lamp's glass globe and blew
out the flame. She settled against the pillow, her eyes heavy
with exhaustion.

She found it impossible to understand her own feelings.
There was an element of strangeness about Donovan that disturbed her, but was it only that? Was it his strangeness? Was it
the fact that she was alone? Or was there something else?

Donovan excited and upset her. Why should that be? She was
supposed to be in mourning, yet she felt no real remorse at the
death of her husband, a man twenty years her senior, a man
whose emotions had turned from lust to menacing without
warning, a man who had stripped her of her dignity in front of
the ranch hands. He'd treated her more like a saloon belle than
a wife.

Moreover, and what was far worse, she was certain Donovan
knew how she felt. Yet he didn't look like a man who would
have known many women. He was remote, and the woman in
her told her that he was lonely.

Her intuition said he was a man who shielded his loneliness

as he did all his feelings. He was ruthless, as ruthless with himself as he would be with others. Oddly, despite his abruptness, she felt more at ease with him than she had with her husband.

She hadn't truly been offended when Donovan had as much as called her a liar about knowing who wanted to scare her off the ranch. She placed her hands over her heart to still the odd fluttering. This was no way for a woman in mourning to feel, no way for any respectable woman to feel.

That might be it. That might be the thing that disturbed her the most. Donovan made her feel like a woman. He made her *feel* . . . yes, that was it. She blushed into the darkness. He made her feel like a female.

How could that be? She'd known him less than twenty-four hours. He'd never touched her or suggested any intimacy.

A queasiness rose inside her throat. She swallowed it down and pressed her hands against her abdomen. This type of thinking was wrong, and she must not allow such thoughts to enter her mind again.

A smoky haze settled over the ranch yard. The barn was now little more than smoldering embers. Donovan pushed through the door and into the bunkhouse. He was surprised to see the old man sitting propped upright against the wall behind his bunk.

"Something on your mind, Teaspoon?"

"I didn't get this old by being stupid, Donovan. The questions you was askin' Miz Dulcie about her husband lead me to believe you might know somethin' more than you're lettin' on."

Donovan sat on the edge of his own bunk and removed his water-soaked socks. He reached inside his rucksack and pulled out a clean pair, pulling them onto his feet. He removed his soot-covered shirt and tossed it aside.

Walking to the wash basin, he emptied the ewer of water

into it and lathered his hands with soap. He scrubbed his arms
and face, his hair, washing the scent of smoke from his body.
Toweling off, he sidestepped the old man's suspicions. "How
long you worked for this outfit, Teaspoon?"

"Nigh on a year. Worked for the Broken W most of my life.
Got all busted up and worn-out from hard work. Then odd
things started happening. First it was a few head of cattle rustled, then more.

"Somebody poisoned the yard dogs, and horses had their ten-
dons slashed. Mean things. One night me and Old Man Winfield
was sittin' on the porch enjoyin' a smoke. Next thing we see
them strange lights a'dancing around the mountains and then the
screamin'." Teaspoon shivered. "Plumb gives me the shivers re-
memberin' it."

Reaching under his pillow, he pulled out a tobacco pouch.
He took a moment to roll a cigarette, light it, and pulled a deep
drag. He exhaled in one long breath. "One night riders rode
through, shot the place up. Killed Winfield and his son. Next
thing I know, Clive Humphrey rides in saying as how he
was the new owner. Said us old codgers weren't no use to him.
Gave us a month's pay and said to skedaddle. I came here and
hired on as bunkhouse cook."

"What happened to the other hands?"

"Humphrey kept those who pledged loyalty to his brand. A
few hired on here at the Circle S. The rest drifted." He finished
off his smoke and stubbed out the butt. "What'er you thinking,
Donovan? That Humphrey killed Slaughter and is now trying to
scare Miz Dulcie off'n the place 'cause she refused to sell to
him?"

"That puzzles me, Teaspoon. Why would a woman of her
quality choose to stay on a ranch without the means to run it?"

The old man shrugged. "Only thing I know is that she's from
New York. Says she has no family, and when the rider from

the Rocking H brought Slaughter's body home, she said she had nothing to go back to."

"Maybe she's running from something—like the law?"

Teaspoon scooted down on the cot and pulled a thin blanket up to his chin. "Cain't say, Donovan. I jest know she's a fine lady, and I'll tromp on any man who tries to hurt her the way Slaughter did."

Donovan tightened his lips. "Did Slaughter hurt her?"

"Saw her sportin' a bruise on her cheekbone once. Used to touch her ungentlemanlike in front of the fellers. If'n you ask me, the owl-hoot who plugged Jack Slaughter did Miz Dulcie a favor."

Silence fell over the room. Donovan bunched his hands into fists, then opened and flexed his fingers.

"Get some shut-eye, Teaspoon. Dawn will get here before we're ready, and there's days of hard work ahead of us."

Chapter Six

Three horsemen entered the yard. Donovan threw a glance at the oldest-looking one, who said something to his companions. Turning their mounts in front of the corral, the men dismounted, flipped the reins of their horses over a post, and walked up the hard-packed dirt toward where Donovan stood on the bunkhouse porch.

Donovan gave the older man's two companions a long, thoughtful glance before he turned his attention to the wrangler. He shifted his eyes on the older man's hard, deeply pocked face. Without seeming to, he looked at the wide, rounded shoulders. His slight pouch indicated a man going to seed. He looked at the single-action Colt revolver in the tied-down holster. The gun rode high on the man's thigh, moving with his rolling gait.

Donovan said, "What's your business, friend?" He noted that the man's eyes failed to hold his own. They were eyes that nurtured a lot of meanness.

"Name's Mayo." He swept his arms wide as a means of introducing his companions. "This here is Hank, and the one missing his front teeth is Sims. Mr. Humphrey from the Rockin' H sent us over to help Miz Slaughter. Didn't know she'd hired on help."

Donovan shrugged. He didn't like their looks and had an uneasy feeling about them. He supposed that came from his years of studying the faces of poker players. And there had been something about Mayo's tone. Donovan reached into his pocket for his tobacco pouch. He shaped a cigarette with elaborate care.

34

"Arrived yesterday. Like most drifters, I stopped in looking for work. Guess it was my lucky day." Donovan twisted the carefully rolled cylinder between his fingers. He ran his tongue across the paper to seal the seam and placed the smoke between his lips.

Mayo reached into his shirt pocket for a match. He swiped it across a Concho on his belt and lifted the flame toward the cigarette. "She hire you to ramrod this outfit?"

"Make any difference if she did?" Donovan glanced toward the other two men.

Mayo said, "Don't reckon it does. Just want to be clear on who's givin' the orders."

Donovan dragged deep on the cigarette, letting the smoke curl around his nostrils. He dropped the butt to the floor and ground it with the toe of his boot.

Already the morning sun was merciless. Sweat stained the shirt of the man named Hank. Donovan noted the beads of sweat on the man's upper lip. A thick stubble of dark brown whiskers covered his lean, muscled jaw. His brown eyes were brooding as he stuck a hand inside his shirt and scratched. His hand came away wet with perspiration.

In Donovan's nostrils was the sour-hot smell of the wrangler, the fetid odor of alcohol and sweat.

"Just so you fellers know, what you do on your off time is your business. On my time, there's no laying about and no boozin'." An edge of irritation rose in him. He glanced over at the house. Then with an almost invisible shrug, his face reflected the tone of his voice. "We're shorthanded. Mrs. Slaughter is joining us on the drive—"

With no front teeth, a whistle followed each word as Sims spoke. "Ever'body knows it's bad luck to bring women on a cattle drive."

"She's the one paying your wages. She'll drive the chuck wagon and do the cooking." Donovan's voice held a challenge.

"Any man who shows her the slightest disrespect will answer to me."

Teaspoon rounded the corner of the bunkhouse, leading two saddled horses. "And the same goes for me. Miz Dulcie is a proper lady. If'n you gotta cuss, keep it outta her earshot; goes fer scratchin' too. Got that clear?"

Anger crawled unpleasantly in the back of Donovan's mind. He didn't like the idea of a woman on a trail drive any more than the others. Still, he owed this woman something for killing her husband and holding the deed to her ranch. He gathered the reins of his gray gelding and, without the use of the stirrup, swung into the saddle. "Teaspoon, you know the lay of the ranch. After we gather the main herd, we'll beat the bushes for strays."

The men followed Donovan's lead and mounted up. They were all turning the horses to head out when Dulcie hurried across the yard toting a war bag. She shielded her eyes against the sun as she handed the bag up to Donovan. "Roast beef sandwiches, a slab of bacon, coffee, a loaf of bread, and beans."

Teaspoon nudged his horse forward. "I'll take that, Miz Dulcie." He wrapped the cord around his saddle horn. He removed his hat and swiped at Mayo. "Better pull them gawking peepers of your'n back in your head."

Donovan's eyes grew hard. He shot Mayo and the other two wranglers a warning glance before he turned his attention to Dulcie. "Remember what I said . . . keep the door bolted at all times. When you come out to tend the animals, bring the shotgun with you. Look for us in two, maybe three days."

With a lift of his hand, he said, "We're burning daylight." He put his horse into a steady trot. He didn't look back but imagined Dulcie standing in the middle of the yard, shading her eyes with an upturned hand as she stared after him.

Donovan and the men followed Teaspoon through a wash in Bryce Canyon. Clumps of sage and creosote bush grew in twisted shapes. Overhead, a pair of eagles dipped and circled, gliding on the wind.

He squinted up at the sky. From the position of the sun, he figured it to be close to noon. There wasn't a cloud to be seen. They were in for a scorcher. Donovan gigged the gray forward, alongside Teaspoon's bay gelding. "How much further?"

Teaspoon didn't answer. He pointed at a small bunch of cows and hauled up on his horse. "Me and Miz Dulcie found these t'other week or so. Rough count estimates 'bout four hundred head."

"Mrs. Slaughter estimated she owned about six hundred. Where would we find the other two hundred?" He looked across at the old cowhand.

Teaspoon removed his hat. He shifted in the saddle as if to ease the pain in his right hip. "Don't rightly know. Like I said before, I hired on as the bunkhouse cook."

The irritation in Donovan's voice was evident. "You mentioned working for a rancher by the name of Winfield. Surely you crossed boundaries when looking for strays."

"Winfield's ranch was way north. Too far to cross onto Circle S land. 'Sides, it was closer to the Rocking H." Teaspoon turned in his saddle to cut a sideways glance at Mayo, the obvious leader of the three Rocking H hands. "Ask one of them."

Donovan twisted around. "Mayo, ride up."

The wrangler goaded his sorrel forward. "Yeah?"

Donovan pointed to the milling herd of scrub cattle. These were scrawny, pied, mottled, long-horned brutes, weaned on cactus, snakeweed, and thistle. Wild and skittish, Donovan didn't look forward to trailing this bunch over two thousand miles of terrain to the nearest railhead. Anything would set these bush poppers into a stampede. He couldn't—wouldn't—risk it with a woman along.

"Teaspoon and Mrs. Slaughter's recent count is four hundred

head. You and your pals back there work all over this range. Got any idea where to find the other two hundred?"

Mayo turned in his saddle. "Hank, Sims . . . haul your lazy carcasses up here."

The two men trotted their horses forward. "Yeah, Mayo?" An abnormally short man with thinning hair streaked with gray spoke. His shoulders and hips were like those of a bull, corded and muscled, and his fists were the size of hams. Donovan figured any man who tangled with this puncher would come out on the losing end.

Mayo said, "Hank, you were out bringing in strays last week; you see anything of the Circle S brand?"

"Yep. Sizable bunch over by Buck Creek. I reported it to Humphrey. He said push 'em back on Circle S land. I did . . . you know cattle. They're more stupid than chickens. One walks, the rest follows."

"How far to Buck Creek?" Donovan wanted to know.

"Five miles, more or less." Sweat stood out on Hank's forehead; his clothes were dusty and his face unshaven.

Donovan didn't respond. He sat staring at the sheer escarpment that rose on three sides around them. It was a natural box, hemmed in by cliffs more than a hundred feet high, its only entrance or exit the way they had come. With ease that belied his stature, he swung out of the saddle.

"Don't reckon they'll wander off. We'll settle long enough to set up camp and rest our ponies. After we've had a bite of grub we'll ride out, do a count, then bring in the stragglers." Donovan watched the Rocking H men dismount, ground-tie their horses, then walk to a spot to squat in a patch of stingy shade.

Mayo said, "Hurry up with them vittles, old man. My innards are stuck to my backbone."

Sims and Hank guffawed at the joke.

Teaspoon lifted the war bag off the saddle horn. Whatever

he was about to say was squashed by the frown knitting Donovan's brows.

Donovan's lean face didn't change, but the hard core in him tightened. His voice was low and firm. "Man isn't worth spit if he doesn't tend to his horse first." His eyes shifted from face to face.

Mayo eased from a squatting position. "What's your point, Donovan?" He hooked his thumbs inside his gunbelt.

Words whistled through Sims' missing teeth. "H-he's right, Mayo, good cowhand always—"

"Shaddup, Sims." Mayo's flat black eyes challenged Donovan. "You never said you was ramrodin' this outfit."

"Now you know. Let's just say that as long as you're eating Mrs. Slaughter's grub and accepting her wages, you'll follow my orders." Donovan measured his words. He stared into Mayo's eyes until the man flinched and turned away.

Donovan's voice deepened with authority. "Just a minute. Although you're on loan from the Rockin' H, let's clear up a few matters: your horse comes first, whatever Mrs. Slaughter asks of you you'll do it without hesitation, and you'll respect her privacy at all times. As long as you ride for the Circle S, I expect loyalty to the brand. Don't ask to get paid until the end of the drive.

"There's six hundred beeves and five men. Unless we can pick up a few extra hands along the trail, we'll work short-handed. That means we'll rotate who rides drag, flank, swing and who scouts a resting place for the night. Any one of you jacklegs get out of hand will answer to me."

Donovan skewered each man with a "you got that?" look. "Teaspoon, I'll tend your horse while you set up the meal."

The old wrangler spat in the dust. He grinned and winked at Donovan before uncorking a canteen and filling the coffee-pot with water.

Chapter Seven

Half an hour later, with the hot breath of the day on their backs, Donovan and the riders flushed cattle from behind mesquite bushes and out of arroyos, and lassoed a bawling steer by its long horns, pulling it from a muddy bog at the end of Buck Creek.

Driving the stragglers together into a bunch, Donovan yelled, "Teaspoon, you and Mayo do a quick count! I'll help Sims and Hank hold the herd in a circle."

Donovan watched the two men urge their ponies in and amongst the herd. Range cattle were as skittish as rabbits. There was always the possibility that the slightest sound would trigger a stampede, and it took only one ornery steer to hook a horse in the belly, sending it and its rider beneath hundreds of trampling hooves.

He didn't enjoy putting the old man in peril, but he trusted his loyalty to Dulcie Slaughter. Donovan paid attention to the way Teaspoon tied a series of knots in the long pigging string he held in his gnarled hands. Donovan figured the old man's count would be truer than Mayo's. His eyes shifted to the pock-faced rider. He, too, used a pigging string to record his count.

Donovan's big gray responded to his master's knee action, working to hold the herd in close. Donovan yelled, "Keep 'em tight!" A black-and-white pied heifer broke from the herd, followed by a couple of steers. "Bring 'em in, Sims!"

The lanky cowboy wheeled his roan. Every horned head

lifted when Sims spurred the pony to catch up with the escapees.

In danger of a stampede, Donovan lifted his arm and made a circular motion with his hand. Hank looked his way and nodded his understanding.

The burly wrangler galloped his horse counterclockwise to Donovan. They used coiled lariats to keep the herd intact. The men rode as close to the bawling beeves as possible, risking danger to themselves and their mounts. One ornery steer with fire in its eyes lowered its head and hooked the tip of its horn inside Hank's pant leg, ripping the material.

Hearing Hank's painful curse over the clacking of horn against horn, Donovan galloped around the circle until face-to-face with the drover. He edged the gray gelding close enough to see the agony-riddled scowl on Hank's face. Donovan kept his eyes trained on the herd. "Hurt bad?"

"I've had worse." Hank sat hunched over and gripped his thigh. Pain deepened the furrows on his sun-baked face, and blood oozed between his fingers.

"Can you hang on till Teaspoon and Mayo are finished?"

Hank gripped the saddle horn, the knuckles on his left hand white. "I ain't no monkey ward, cowboy."

Donovan cocked a sideways grin. He focused on the two men doing the count. He hadn't realized how tight he'd held himself until the old man and Mayo eased their horses from the middle of the herd.

Sims pushed the three escaping stragglers back to join the bunch. Donovan called the positions. "Sims on drag. Hank, ride swing, and Mayo, flank."

Donovan shook out the loop on his lariat and lassoed a blue-brindled steer around the horns. "Get 'im on the other side, Teaspoon."

Without question, the old wrangler opened up a loop and

threw with an expert arm. He spat before he spoke. "Reckon you gonna train Ol' Blue here as lead steer."

Donovan nodded, thankful the wall-eyed steer seemed satisfied to amble along at a placid pace.

The hours dragged on as the great clock in the sky crossed the mountain summit and wheeled westward. Bandannas kept Donovan and the drovers from choking on the clouds of dust.

Above the querulous bawls of irritated steers, the men steadily pushed until the herd collectively followed behind Ol' Blue.

"He's gonna make a fine lead steer. Don't you reckon?" The dust-caked bandanna muffled Teaspoon's words.

The brindled steer lowered its head, planted its front legs, and balked. Donovan lashed out with a swift kick to the animal's shoulder. "If he don't make a liar out of you first, Teaspoon."

The balking steer nearly yanked the old wrangler out of the saddle. "Consarn yer ornery hide. Git on up there, you sorry bag o' bones."

Working as a team, Donovan and Teaspoon forced the animal through a stand of tall chaparral for some distance. Donovan glanced to where Hank rode swing position. The drover wore an ashen mask.

"Hank's leg needs tendin'. How much farther to the main herd?"

Teaspoon used his toe to prod the brindled steer. "Give a listen."

Donovan leaned forward in the saddle until he made out lowing. The plodding steer picked up its pace. "Let's get the ropes off this critter, Teaspoon."

"You got it, Ramrod."

Donovan's voice rang out, "Let 'em run." He moved to the right-swing position, well out of the line of danger.

Voices yelled in unison, and the riders streamed behind the spooked animals.

Blowing and snorting, the animals' pounding feet were followed by more and more until the last tired cow scrambled into the arroyo to join four hundred grazing beeves. Evening was pushing scarlet and gray by the time Donovan and the wranglers settled the entire herd.

Over a small fire of dried wood, Teaspoon set about frying slices of sowbelly. He mixed up a batter of cornmeal and water to fry a batch of spoonbread. While the coffee simmered, he lifted a canteen and a sewing kit from his saddlebag and walked over to where Hank nursed his injured leg.

Glancing over his shoulder, Teaspoon said, "Sims, if'n you want supper, you best turn them corn dodgers before they burn. And don't let the coffee boil over." Teaspoon grumbled under his breath, "I'm too danged old for all this ruckusing around." Then he said aloud, "And mind you don't drop none o' them dodgers in the dirt."

"Quit yer bellyaching, old man." Hank grimaced, the pain evident on his face.

"Donovan and Mayo's nursemaidin' cows, and I only got two hands. Now you kin let me doctor up that wound or you kin let it fester. Makes no never mind to me if'n we have to whack off yer leg when gangrene sets in."

"What's in the canteen?"

Teaspoon uncapped the container. "Snake pi'zen."

"Gimme a swig. Need something to take the edge off the hurtin'."

Hank fairly snatched the canteen from the old cowchaser's hands. A shuddering grimace accompanied each slug he chugged down.

"Go easy. This here stuff'll make you drunker'n a cross-eyed billy goat." Teaspoon's irritation was evident when he grabbed the canteen away and commanded Hank to roll over on his side.

He conceded the injury to the drover's hip was long and angry but not deep enough for stitching. "Better grit yer teeth, 'cause this is gonna burn hotter'n a branding iron." He trickled the rotgut into the laceration made by the steer's horn.

Hank sucked in a trembling breath and blew it out with a steady and imaginative string of curses.

Teaspoon popped the cap back on the canteen. He tossed the sewing kit to the moaning drover. "I'll tend anybody what needs tendin', but I ain't stitching up their britches. No sirree."

Deep in thought, Donovan rode into the camp. With the herd settled in for the night, there was little concern about a stampede. Weary from the long day, he stepped out of the saddle and loosened the girth strap. Mayo swung his horse alongside. "We gonna keep these ponies saddled for the night?"

"Nah. Unless something out of the ordinary spooks 'em, the rope gate ought to keep the herd inside the gulch till we can move 'em out in the morning."

"Good. My stomach's talkin' to me." Mayo lifted the saddle off the gelding's sweaty back. He picked a spot next to the campfire and dropped his gear. He squatted and reached for the coffeepot.

Donovan joined him. Both men accepted the plates that Teaspoon had filled with corn dodgers, fried sowbelly, and beans. Spoons scraping against metal plates and loud snores emitting from the wounded drover mingled with lowing beeves and yipping coyotes.

Sopping up the last of the bean broth and stuffing his mouth with the ball of corn bread, Donovan chewed thoughtfully. He handed his plate to Teaspoon and then offered his cup for a refill. "Other than scaring the coyotes with that loud ruckus, how's Hank?"

Teaspoon scooped up a fistful of sand and let it sift through his hand onto Donovan and Mayo's dirty plates. He took the rag from his shoulder and wiped the utensils clean, stuffing them back inside the war bag. "Told him that snake pi'zen had a kick to it. His head'll hurt worse than that itty-bitty scratch on his leg."

Donovan chuckled. "I take it he'll live."

"For a while anyways."

A thin and distant sound caught Donovan's attention. He peered through the darkness, listening. "Sounds like we're about to have a visitor."

Keeping his voice low, Teaspoon said, "Only two kind of men ride around in the dead of night—them that's lost and them who're up to no good. What with night riders burning Miz Dulcie's barn, I don't rightly think whoever's out there is paying us a social call."

Sims chimed in, "Could be rustlers."

Donovan considered greeting the rider with an invitation to step down for a cup of coffee. On the other hand, what if Sims was right and the rider was scouting the camp with intentions of stealing the herd?

Unfurling from a squat, he stepped away from the campfire and into the shadows. "You boys act natural. Our visitor is in for a little surprise." Using the darkness as a shield, he eased toward the thud of hoofbeats. As if he'd used a springboard, he leapt forward, tackling the rider.

Donovan's weight and size was no match for the slight figure he'd knocked out of the saddle. The startled horse whinnied and reared. Donovan grabbed the kicking, flailing figure by the scruff of the shirt. He reared back his arm and before letting loose with a meaty fist, a frightened contralto voice squeaked, "Mrs. Slaughter sent me."

The sound of Dulcie's name brought Teaspoon to his feet.

He scrambled to where Donovan held the trembling boy. "Tobias, somethin' wrong with Miz Dulcie?"

The boy shook free of Donovan's grip. He brushed dirt from his shirt. "No sir, Mr. Teaspoon. Everything's fine at the ranch. Mrs. Slaughter is fine—"

"Well, get on it with it, boy. Don't stand there flappin' yer jaws. If everything's fine, then why'd she send you out here?"

"Me and Pa rode over to see what all the smoke was about. Mrs. Slaughter explained about night riders burning her barn, and how you and her new ramrod and men from the Rockin' H was out rounding up the herd.

"When she said how shorthanded she was, I asked Pa if I could hire on, with her approval, of course. And he said, that is, my pa said that since I was sixteen, he reckoned I was full grown enough to take on a man's job."

Donovan pulled at his bottom lip. It was bad enough to have a woman along on the drive. The thought of wet-nursing a boy didn't sit well with him.

"You ever been on a drive before, boy?"

"My name ain't boy, sir. It's Tobias Jenkins. Most everyone calls me Toby. No, sir, I ain't never been on a drive before, but I know how to work cows."

Teaspoon spat a stream of tobacco. "I've known this boy since he was knee-high to a grasshopper, Donovan. He comes from a good and honest family. What he don't know, he'll learn."

Donovan's blue eyes scanned the boy from head to toe. Tall and wiry, the kid looked as if a good puff of wind would blow him right out of the saddle. Donovan offered the boy his hand. "Aw right. We can use another rider."

The notion that had been forming in Donovan's head all day finally came to fruition. With almost six hundred head of range-crazy cows, working shorthanded, and with a woman and a boy to look after, he'd made his decision.

"Gather round, men."

"By the look on your face, I'd say you got somethin' stuck in yer craw, Donovan." Sweat trickled down the old wrangler's wrinkled face.

Donovan harrumphed. "Odds seem to be hundred to one against us. Scrub cattle. By the time we trail 'em a thousand miles to Kansas there won't be enough meat on them to bring two bits on the hoof. Not only that, with Indians and wide-loopers looking to rustle a few head here and there, we'll be lucky to get to the stockyards with five hundred head. Then at best we'll trail in behind the Rockin' H herd and any other outfits already ahead of us. You all know top dollar goes to those who run 'em first.

"Next thing on my mind: Can Mrs. Slaughter hold up under the rigors of eating a thousand miles of dust, fording rivers, heat so hot it'll scorch your eyeballs, rattlers big as a man's arm, and worse . . . stampede?"

A coyote yipped; across the night another answered. Hearing the forlorn and lonely sound, Donovan equated it to his own life. He shifted on his haunches. He'd carefully folded the deed to the ranch and hidden it inside the parfleche that hung around his neck and out of sight beneath his shirt. Maybe he should hand it to Teaspoon and light out, get on with his search for the last man on his list. He had no ties to the woman. No ties except making her a widow.

The old wrangler's voice roused Donovan from his thoughts. "Where'd you go? Yer eyes took on a far-off look, like you were deep thinking."

"Yep. Deep thinking is right. We're not drivin' to Kansas."

"The dickens you say!" Mayo nearly choked on his coffee.

"You ain't thinking on pushin' them beeves up to Nebraskey, are you?" Teaspoon spat a wad and swiped his shirtsleeve across his mouth.

Donovan waited until the men had absorbed his declaration.

"Nope. Fort Apache. If we push the herd through the Superstitions, it's two hundred miles. Without incident, we'll make it in less than three months. That's a whole lot shorter than near a year to Kansas."

Mayo poked at the campfire embers with a stick. "Why Fort Apache?"

"No competition. The army will buy every head of stock for the Indian Agency to supply to the reservations. Starving Indians don't much care about the breed of cattle or how puny they are. Army money is as good as any."

A low hiss from the pock-faced drover caused Teaspoon to break his silence. "What s'matter with you, Mayo? His plan is sound as I ever did hear. Cattle depend on good grazin' 'long the trail. It's July and with ten thousand beeves already ahead of us, there won't be a blade or bush big enough for a grasshopper to squat on."

Sims shot up from the ground like somebody had lit the soles of his boots on fire. Words whistled through his front missing teeth. "I ain't going. Nope. Count me out. I ain't going." He snatched off his hat and slapped it against his thigh, then jammed it back on his head to show his irritation. "'Sides, there's ghosts in them mountains."

"Shaddup, Sims." Hank's annoyance at being awakened was evident when he sat up, scratched his hands through his hair, and growled. "You're squawkin' loud 'nuf to wake the dead. Ain't no such things as ghosts."

"What the hell are you talking about, Sims?" Donovan's words were clipped and harsh.

The lanky cowboy's eyes seemed to bounce around nervously as he glanced from companion to companion. "One night I was up in the mountains huntin' fer strays. Had my old dog with me. It was hotter'n Hades, it was. A cold wind come up out of nowhere. That's when the screams started. My old dog let out one long howl . . . like he knew something evil was out there. That po' old cur tucked his tail 'tween his legs and lit out like he'd been peppered with birdshot. Ain't seen hide nor hair of him since." Sims shuddered. He rubbed his hands up and down his arms as if he'd experienced a sudden chill. "I tell you, there's ghosts in them mountains."

"Ah, shut your blatterin', Sims. You sound like a simpleton." Teaspoon guffawed. He lifted his hands, wiggled his fingers toward the wrangler's face, and *hoo*ed in a quavering voice. He guffawed again. "Like Hank said, there ain't no sech thing as spooks."

Donovan's voice seemed to echo over the silence that befell the camp. "Any man who wants out, collect his gear . . . now. I'll not waste anymore of Mrs. Slaughter's money or food on cowards."

He cut his eyes toward the kid who sat white-faced, knees drawn to his chin. "Toby?"

The boy stopped hugging his knees and met Donovan's eyes. "My family's depending on the bonus Mrs. Slaughter promised at the end of the trail. 'Sides, my pa didn't raise me to be no yellow-bellied sapsucker."

Donovan quirked a grin and a wink at young Tobias Jenkins. His gut told him the boy would grow into a fine man. "Mayo, Hank . . . you boys ridin' back to the Rockin' H?"

After a brief glance and a nod as if to signal their mutual agreement, Mayo said, "Mr. Humphrey sent us to help the little lady for long as need be. We're stickin'."

"You've made your position clear, Sims. Collect your gear and ride out." Donovan spoke with authority.

"Might's well keep on ridin', Sims. Once Humphrey gets wind of this, you're good as fired." The pock-faced wrangler skewed a frown at the man.

Sims sucked wind through the toothless gap between his lips. "This shore is an uncivil outfit. Blast it all, I ain't apologizin' for nothing, but I'll stick."

Donovan's voice was ice. "Fair warning, Sims. If you turn yellow on the trail, it won't be ghosts you have to worry about. Savvy?"

Sims looked freshly stricken. Even in the firelight, Donovan saw the man's guzzle work up and down. "Ah, anything you say, Trail Boss."

Unsmiling, Donovan crossed his legs and folded his body to sit Indian fashion against his saddle. He pulled the pouch from his shirt pocket and rolled a cigarette. He lifted a stick from the fire and lit the tobacco. He dragged deep, exhaling and letting the smoke curl around his face. A woman, a boy, an arthritic old cowpuncher, a chucklehead afraid of spooks, and two men of questionable character—what the hell had he gotten himself into?

Chapter Eight

Daybreak came with a redness in the east. It tinged the mountains, rocks, sage, and grass plain. Energy filled Donovan as he peered at the outlines of pale bluffs, not so vague and ghostlike in the morning light.

"Toby, hightail it to the ranch. Help Mrs. Slaughter load the chuck wagon and with anything else she needs. Tell her we're bringing the herd in and to be ready to pull out day after tomorrow before the sun breaks dawn."

"Yes, sir." The boy swallowed the last of his breakfast and tossed the plate to Teaspoon. In two shakes he swung into the saddle, his pony kicking up dust as he lit out.

"Hank, you and Mayo stay in the camp and keep an eye on the herd. Sims, you'll go with Teaspoon and me to round up the horses we spotted yesterday."

Hank rose stiffly to his feet. He rested his weight on his good leg. "Already told you, I ain't no monkey ward, cowboy. I can ride."

A frown knotted Donovan's brow. "No room for cripples on a drive. A few hours of ease is all you'll get this morning. Soon as we round up a good remuda, you'll get your share of saddle pounding."

Mayo's calculating glance toward Hank caused Donovan to search his memory for something familiar about these two, but he came up empty. Maybe it was Donovan's Comanche instinct that touched his spine with a kind of chill.

Maybe it was the way Mayo kept brushing his hands against his gunbutt or the way Hank bore himself, but here were two men he'd bet were more gunmen than cowpunchers.

His senses on edge, Donovan's voice bristled. "Soon as we've cut out twenty or so head of horses, I'll send Sims to help you push the cattle up behind the remuda. Once we get 'em started they'll settle down, and with twenty miles to the ranch these bags of hides'll be too weary to stampede."

Mechanically he hauled himself into the saddle. His eyes flashed toward Teaspoon and Sims. "Let's move."

Mayo swung around, his dark eyes narrowing. He waited a scant second before he strode to his saddlebag and lifted the flap. He dug through the insides until his fingers closed over a small, round cylinder.

Facing the lip above Cutler Gap, he extended his arms, holding the mirror toward the sun. Using the reflective surface as a signal, he flashed three times in rapid succession.

"Reckon they seen you?" Hank's voice roughened.

"Know in a minute."

Both men kept their eyes trained toward the mountain. "C'mon," Mayo growled. "What're they doing up there—sleeping?"

Hank indicated with his arm. "There it is." He counted, "One . . . two . . . three—" until he reached five. "Who you reckon'll ride down?"

Mayo tucked the mirror back into the saddlebag. "Don't make no difference as long as he gets here and gone before Donovan runs the remuda past."

"We'll need to be careful around that idiot Sims." Hank unbuckled his gunbelt and let it slide to the ground. He lowered his britches to look at the painful scratch. He winced at the red and festered area. "Sure hope I don't get blood pi'zen."

"You're too ornery." Mayo cupped his hands over his eyes and squinted. "Don't know who it is, but he's ridin' in."

Rebuckling his belt, Hank, too, squinted.

"You stay here, Hank. I'll ride out and meet him."

"What about Donovan?"

"We got plenty of time before him and the others get the horses rounded up and cut out a string for the remuda."

Hank rubbed his leg as he limped over to perch on a boulder where he could keep a lookout for Donovan and follow Mayo's direction as he rode out of camp.

To the left the land sloped down to meet the base of another set of hills, and to the other side was higher ground dotted with trees and laced with trails leading back to the lip of the mountain. Mayo was halfway across the basin when the other rider appeared.

The hoof falls stopped. A narrow-shouldered man with a face that reminded Mayo of a weasel, Vesper Bonner slouched in the saddle alongside the base of the bluff, having come down a trail concealed by a sweep of rock.

"Howdy, Mayo. Been watching all the activity. What's doing?"

"Mrs. Slaughter's hired herself a ramrod. He's got the bright idea to trail the beeves through the Superstitions. Thought Old Man Humphrey oughta know."

"How come you didn't ride over to Rockin' H and tell him yerself?"

Mayo regarded the gunman intently. "And what's my reasoning gonna be to the new ramrod, that I gotta go check in with my boss like I was a snivelin' Sunday school kid?"

"Ain't no call in gettin' riled." Wiping his mouth with the back of his hand, Vesper said, "Must've been the new ramrod who plugged Dink."

"Yeah, heard night riders paid the little lady a visit. Didn't know it was you and Dink. He hurt bad?"

"Bad 'nuf. We buried him last night."

Mayo squinted pensively. "Can't say it's a great loss to society."

"Yeah, well, maybe he didn't count for much, but he was my friend and I aim to avenge his death."

"Who's up there with you?"

"Smitty."

"One of you ride in to let Humphrey know that Donovan is moving the herd day after tomorrow before dawn. Also, the woman is driving the chuck wagon."

"A woman . . . on a drive? Now don't that beat all." Vesper smacked his lips together as if savoring the last of a tasty meal. "She's a looker . . . lots could happen when a woman wanders off from camp to tend to her possibles."

"You know how Humphrey feels about the woman. Best keep those ideas locked up. Just ride in and ask the boss if he wants to play it the same as with the other herds, and I don't care how you get word back to me, just don't get caught. My gut tells me Donovan has enough Ind'an in him to smell trouble before it comes."

"Anything else I need to tell the old man about this here Donovan?"

"Yeah. He don't scare easy. Put Dink in a hole, didn't he?"

Vesper shrugged. "How many riding with this new ramrod?"

Mayo ticked off the names. "Not counting me and Hank—four."

"Easy pickin's."

"Just make sure you don't get gun crazy and put me and Hank in your sights."

The excited, wall-eyed expression on Vesper's face created a knot in Mayo's gut. His top lip curled into a snarl. "Report in to Humphrey. It's his range they're crossin'. And with him having a soft spot for the woman . . . mebbe he'll charge her a toll for crossing his range . . . mebbe not."

"Yeah, and mebbe the herd and crew will disappear jest like t'others."

The pounding of hooves and high whinnies mingled with the loud bawling of cattle drew Mayo's attention. "Hell's fire." He stared toward the camp. "Thought it'd take most of the day to round up a string for the remuda. Hank can't handle four hundred head of range-crazy beeves by himself."

Glancing over his shoulder, Mayo swung his horse around. "Don't use the mirror to signal. It'll only draw attention."

"How'll I get word to you from the boss?"

Mayo gripped the saddle horn and planted his feet in the stirrups to keep the fidgeting horse from dumping him. "When I figure it out, you'll know. Now git on outta here. And stay out of sight. Boss sent Sims with me and Hank to help the woman."

Vesper expelled an obscene sound. "Sims . . ." The gunman patted his holster. "Leave him to me."

Mayo resisted the urge to spur the gelding. He had time to casually trot the long-legged sorrel back to camp before Donovan and the boys ran the string of horses past the camp.

Knowing a tired animal might stumble, Mayo wasn't ready to die. Not today.

Donovan pulled away from the string of horses. He barreled into camp. The gray reared and pawed the air, dancing on his back legs. Donovan yelled to Hank, "Put a lasso on Ol' Blue!" He turned his attention to Mayo, who still sat in the saddle. "We'll move the herd out easy. Spent too much time rounding 'em up for them to stampede and scatter from here to yonder." Then, speaking softly, Donovan settled the excited gray gelding.

With the way Hank listed in the saddle, Donovan figured the man's leg was in a bad way. He watched the brindled steer dip its head to avoid the noose Hank tossed. The rope missed its mark. Hank coiled it in and opened the loop. Twirling it overhead this time, his swing was true. The noose settled over the pair of long horns. Donovan rode up and slapped a coiled riata across the animal's hindside. Bawling its protest, the steer followed Hank at a lope.

The boxed canyon came alive with commotion as restless cattle boiled to freedom through the narrow opening, with Donovan and Mayo riding drag.

With the herd on the move and riding hard, Donovan and Mayo switched between swing and flank positions. After five miles at a steady pace, the cattle settled into a shuffling walk. Fifteen miles later steers and horses alike waded into Mossy Creek to cool their sweat-soaked hides and quench their thirst.

Donovan and the cowpunchers lined along the bank, allowing their mounts to plunge their muzzles into the cold clear water and drink. He stepped down from the saddle and squatted. With the reins draped over his arm, he bent low, cupped his hand, and splashed cool water over his face. Removing his bandanna, he soaked the cloth and wrapped it around the back of his sweaty neck. "Sims, you and Mayo drive the horses into the corral. We'll leave the cattle here. We've run the edge off 'em for the time being."

With a nod for an answer, Mayo and Sims reined their dust-covered horses from the creek.

The pasty mask on Hank's face concerned Donovan. "Hank, follow Teaspoon to the bunkhouse so he can look at your leg."

The old man and the drover let exhaustion speak for them as they turned their mounts toward the ranch yard. Donovan hauled his aching body into the saddle and followed.

Chapter Nine

Dulcie stood on the front porch, one hand lifted to shade her eyes from the sun. The heat seemed especially oppressive on this sun-scorched July morning. She quickly buttoned the front of her dress even as rivulets of perspiration trickled down her sides. She fanned vigorously with her hand, trying to scare up a breeze.

A mounting sense of excitement continued to build as she watched men, cattle, and horses steadily moving toward the creek, her eyes searching for one man in particular.

For all her surface bravado, she couldn't help the feelings of uncertainty and something akin to fear, making her wish fervently to be anywhere else but here. She wasn't a coward, she told herself. Even joining the drive seemed worse than the ordeal of leaving New York, marrying Jack Slaughter, and now an uncertain future. Well, it was over, he was dead, and all she had to do was face the next challenge. What had her father said? She searched for the memory of his words.

Courage. Once you faced what you thought of as an obstacle as squarely as you would face a challenge, it would never seem insurmountable. And yet, as Dulcie stood on the porch, everything about her life seemed to have become hazy and unreal, like a blurred scene watched in a dream.

Perhaps it was the heat, or perhaps it was the secret she carried inside her that caused her to reach out and hold on to the porch post. She blinked away the dizziness, gulped in a few breaths of air, and pasted a smile on her face.

"I didn't expect you back so soon, Donovan."

"Mornin', Mrs. Slaughter. Toby around?"

"We tried hitching my mare and my husband's, um, my late husband's horse to the chuck wagon, but they fought the traces so hard that Toby said he'd ride over to get a pair of wagon-broke horses from his father. I expect he'll—"

Her focus shifted toward Teaspoon and the man hunched over in the saddle as the two rode toward the bunkhouse. "Is Hank ill?"

"Not exactly. Steer horned him in the leg."

She gathered her skirts. "I'll bring hot water, bandages, and tincture of iodine."

"'Preciate it." Donovan turned his horse, then wheeled back. "When did you say Toby will return?"

"Today . . . this evening." Not able to pinpoint an exact time, she shrugged and hurried to the shady interior of the house.

Hank staggered sideways, gripping his leg just above the knee. Teaspoon buckled under the man's weight as he tried to maintain his balance.

Donovan flipped the reins over the hitchpost and gripped Hank under the right armpit, then saw the dark, spreading patch on the pant leg. With Donovan and Teaspoon supporting him, Hank clumsily hobbled up the steps. Expelling a painful groan, he slipped into blackness. Lugging the unconscious man inside the bunkhouse, they dragged Hank across the room and laid him on the nearest bunk. Dulcie bounded inside and crossed the room with a kettle of hot water in one hand and a canvas bag in the other. Donovan noted that she'd had the good sense to put an apron over her dress. He looked down at the passed out man, now flinching with delirium. Sliding the knife from its sheath, Donovan ripped upward, opening the pant leg around the wound. At her gasp, he regarded Dulcie's pale face.

"Teaspoon, get her out of here before she faints." Donovan straightened from his work and took the kettle and bag of medicinal needs from Dulcie.

Putting one hand out to signal she didn't need help, she placed the other hand to her mouth and rushed out the door.

Donovan felt his own throat constrict as fetid odor filled his nostrils. "A few more days and he'd lose this leg."

Teaspoon rummaged around in the bag and lifted out a bottle marked tincture of iodine and one of sulfur powder. "Gonna take a heap more'n this to kill the pi'zen."

"You got any ideas?"

The old man set the bottles aside. He scratched his head. "I ain't 'zactly no doctor, but this here wound needs cauterizing—only way to kill the infection. What we need is a hot brandin' iron."

Looking down at the man on the bunk, Donovan mulled Teaspoon's statement. "Take too long to heat one up." He thought for a moment. "I have an idea. You clean out the wound."

"Whatcha gonna do?"

"Saw an army doctor do this once. 'Course, the soldier ended up dying."

Teaspoon harrumphed.

Donovan lifted three cartridges from his gunbelt. Using the edge of his knife, he skillfully removed the caps and set them aside. "You ready?"

Teaspoon's eyes shifted from Donovan's hands to Hank's leg. "You ain't, uh, gonna do what I'm thinking, are you?"

"It's either this or let him die a one-legged man."

Hank roused around. He drew in a deep breath and mumbled incoherently. Donovan said to him, "We're going to cauterize the wound, Hank. You up to the pain?"

Drenched in sweat, his eyes glassy, Hank answered, "Gimme somethin' to bite on."

Donovan instructed Teaspoon to unbuckle Hank's belt.

When the old man placed the leather strap between Hank's teeth, Donovan said, "Chomp down hard."

Hank nodded. He closed his eyes.

"Can you hold him, Teaspoon?"

"Ain't no young feller no more. Hang on a second." Teaspoon strode to the door and yelled, "Mayo . . . Sims . . . haul yer carcasses in here . . . on the double."

When the two men entered the bunkhouse, Teaspoon said, "Sims, you hold on to Hank's legs. Me and Mayo'll bear down on his shoulders."

"Wait . . . wait. I need a drink." Hank garbled the words through clenched teeth.

Donovan nodded, and Teaspoon walked over and groped under his bunk. He drew out a long-necked bottle. The pulled cork made a popping sound. He removed the belt from Hank's mouth and lifted his head with one hand while using the other to hold the bottle to the man's lips.

Pulling a deep swig, Hank choked and sputtered. Whiskey dribbled from the corner of his mouth. "Take it easy there, pardner."

Before corking the bottle, Teaspoon tilted his head back and rewarded himself with a chug. He offered a swig to Mayo, who accepted, and then to Donovan, who said, "Afterwards."

When the men were in position, Donovan sent a silent question to Hank. The man nodded. His jaws clamped down on the belt.

Not wanting to prolong the man's agony, Donovan pulled up a chair and scooted as close to the bunk as possible. He used the fingers of one hand to spread the angry wound wide. With great care, he lined the infected area with gunpowder from the first opened cartridge. He was careful not to spill any of the powder on Hank's clothes, even taking time to brush a bit of spilled granules off his skin and into the opening.

When the area was filled from tip to tip, he brushed his own hands against his denims lest a flash set his hands on fire. Satisfied they were clean, he reached inside his shirt pocket and removed a match.

The muscles in his back tightened. He didn't take time to question whether what he was doing was right or wrong. Using his thumbnail, he flicked the tip of the sulfur match and watched it flare. Pursing his lips, he eyed the men holding Hank. His stare seemed to admonish them to hold tight and not let him jerk around.

He was unaware that Dulcie and Toby stood in the doorway, both of them gaping and speechless.

He touched the match flame to the gunpowder and like a dynamite fuse, the fine particles danced and burned its way from one end of the wound to the other.

Hank's scream permeated the room until his eyes rolled back into his head and then all was silent.

Chapter Ten

Donovan accepted the drink he'd earlier refused. The whiskey burned its way down his gullet and into the pit of his stomach. He grimaced and blew out a breath.

"This is pure rotgut, Teaspoon."

The old man chuckled. "It'll either kill you or cure what ails you, that's for danged sure."

"I'll leave you to bind up Hank's leg."

Dulcie stepped forward. "No, I'm fine now. I'll do it."

Spitting like a hissing cat, Teaspoon said, "No, ma'am. Ain't fit for a lady like yerself to be looking at a man's near nakedness." He shooed her away. "I'll tend to it."

"Then what can I do to help?"

Donovan stepped forward. "We could all use a decent meal, Mrs. Slaughter."

"Of course. I have a huge pot of stew, yeast bread, and coffee prepared. When you've washed up, all of you come to the house." She lifted her skirts and set off to place the food on the table.

Donovan focused on the boy. "Toby, you bring those wagon horses?"

"Well, not exactly."

"What's that supposed to mean?"

"Pa didn't want to risk harm to any of his Belgians. He sent Homer and Plato instead."

Not understanding, Donovan skewed his brow into a frown. "Who the hell are they?"

" 'They' are mules. Sturdy, well-muscled, and if treated right will pull all day and half the night."

"Already inside the corral?"

"Yes, sir."

"Good. I'll see that Mrs. Slaughter pays your pa for the mules. C'mon, the horses need tending." His boot heel scraped the floor as he followed the boy. "Sims, you and Mayo . . ."

Sims chuckled. "Yeah, we know, Ramrod."

The men left Teaspoon to bind up Hank's leg while they ambled out to take care of their horses.

Donovan had no way of knowing that Hank's injury had unwittingly solved Mayo's problem of communicating with Clive Humphrey.

Turning their horses into the corral, Mayo said, "Don't look like Hank'll be joining us on the drive."

"No, and that's a problem. Not only does it leave us short a man, we can't leave him here and he's not fit to travel."

"How 'bout after I grab a bite to eat, I hitch up the buckboard and drive Hank back to the Rockin' H? While I'm there, I'll explain the situation to Mr. Humphrey and see if he can spare a couple of men." Mayo casually rolled a smoke and stuck it between his lips. He accepted a light from Donovan.

Donovan lit his own cigarette. He inhaled deep, considering Mayo's proposal. Afternoon had come, but the sun was obscured by billowing thunderclouds. Thunder rumbled like the boom of far-off cannons. His eyes riveted toward the cattle searching for signs of a stampede. Some cattle milled; others lay placidly chewing their cud.

"How long will it take you to get there and back?"

Mayo dropped the spent butt to the ground and toed it out. "Three hours by buckboard."

"Saddle one of the horses from the remuda for the trip back. Might as well start riding the buck out of 'em."

"Anything you say, Ramrod."

"Be on your way as soon as you grab some grub." The short hairs on the back of Donovan's neck prickled, leaving him puzzled. "You can leave the buckboard, but bring back the mules first thing in the morning. Express Mrs. Slaughter's gratitude to your boss for the extra hands."

Before sundown, Donovan helped lift a supine Hank into the back of the buckboard. Dulcie tucked a quilt around his shivering body, and Teaspoon handed him a bottle. "Just a little something to take the edge off."

Mayo flapped the reins. "Hie up there, mules!" He lifted his hand and, without looking back, waved.

Halting the mules, Mayo tested the night with his senses. At the bottom of the grade before him was a wide grassy floor. In the middle distance was the Rocking H's sprawl of buildings. Clive Humphrey's house was two storied with twin dormers at its top and a wide veranda gracing three of its sides. A picket fence surrounding the yard set off the residence from the corrals, the barn, and the bunkhouses nearby.

Judging the placement of the moon, Mayo figured it was closed to midnight. The bunkhouses were dark and filled with men sleeping off a full day's work. A single light showed in the main house, in the right front room on the first floor. This, Mayo knew, was Humphrey's study. The rancher would be staying up late with paperwork of some kind.

A bitter envy nagged at him. It wasn't right that one man should own so much.

Hank groaned. "How much farther?"

Without answering, Mayo clucked the mules forward. Entering the yard at a plodding pace, he hauled up in front of the house. The chassis squeaked when he stepped down from the wagon. He tethered the team to the hitching rail outside the white picket fence.

A low growl greeted him, then another. "Shaddup, dog."

The bull mastiff issued a deeper warning. "Bite me and you're dead." Mayo unholstered his revolver. He yelled out, "Humphrey, call off your dog . . . Humphrey!"

Clive Humphrey was a heavyset man with thick, graying hair and a ruddy face sparked by alert brown eyes. He opened the door and held up a lantern. A grating rasp called, "Who's out here?"

A snarl rumbled in the dog's throat.

"It's me, Mayo."

Humphrey admonished the dog. "Quiet, Brutus." Holding the lantern higher, he said, "Why are you here this time of night and driving a buckboard?"

"Never mind that. You heard from Vesper?"

"I have. He said something about Mrs. Slaughter hiring a ramrod and that you'd get in touch with me about the details."

"Yeah. Didn't know how I was going to pull it off until Hank got himself hooked by a steer. Got him in the back of the wagon. He's in a bad way."

Humphrey reached down and grabbed the dog's collar. "I'll lock Brutus in the shed while you drive Hank over to the bunkhouse. Soon as you get him settled, we'll talk."

Minutes later, Mayo had roused the cook to help him get Hank into a bunk. He'd unhitched the mules and led them inside the corral, then strode to the house.

He rapped once, turned the doorknob, and entered without invitation. Then he moved toward the lighted room and found Humphrey sitting behind a massive oak desk in a wood-paneled study, idly looking over a ledger book.

Humphrey flicked his eyes toward an overstuffed chair. "Sit down, Mayo."

Picking up a coffeepot, he poured two cups and laced the coffee with brandy. He offered a cup to Mayo. "Now, what's this about Mrs. Slaughter hiring herself a man and trailing her cattle across the Superstition Mountains?"

The unnatural timbre of Humphrey's voice irritated Mayo. It sounded as if the man needed to hawk up a wad to clear his throat.

Weary from a day's work and the long trip to the ranch, Mayo finished the brew in one long gulp and held the cup out for a refill. "She's hired herself a man, all right. My take is he could stare down the devil without flinchin'."

"Professional man . . . bounty hunter?"

"Not a bounty hunter. He don't carry the stink of death on him. I'd say more like a gun for hire." This time Mayo sipped and seemed to savor the expensive liquid before swallowing. "That ol' hired hand of hers, Teaspoon, said Donovan rode in lookin' for work. She hired him."

"According to Vesper, this Donovan is the one who killed Dink."

"Guess so."

Humphrey laced his hands together. For a moment, he concentrated on flexing his fingers. "Donovan . . . Donovan. It seems I should know that name. What's your take on the man?"

"He's smart, knows cattle and horses. Might've been in the war—seems used to givin' orders and 'spects 'em to get carried out."

Shoving away from the chair and padding over to the window, Mayo stared out at the night he'd just driven through and then turned to the rancher, his mouth a thin line. "Somethin' else. I'd stake my life that Donovan is part Comanche."

"Indian? What makes you think so?"

"The way he's built and walks and sits a horse. And the way he looks right through a man."

"Hmm." Humphrey nodded plaintively. "His heritage doesn't concern me. White or red, all men die when a bullet hits its mark."

"What about the woman? She's going on the drive."

"So it is true. I didn't believe Vesper when he told me."

Humphrey rose to pace back and forth. He looked lazily over the paintings that lined the wall, the mounted animal heads and the bookshelves. "Although I have great personal interest in Mrs. Slaughter, that does not exempt her from paying tolls to cross my range with her cattle, like everyone else."

Humphrey held up his hand to stop Mayo from speaking. "However, I'll ride out and endear myself to the pretty lady by inviting her to dinner and waiving the toll."

"What about the herd and the men?"

"I only said I was waiving the toll. I'll send word to Vesper to get ready. Then while I'm entertaining Mrs. Slaughter, the 'ghosts' that haunt Superstition Mountain will appear, and by the time I escort her back to the campsite, she'll never know what became of the men or her cattle. *Poof*—disappeared into thin air."

Humphrey's raspy, insidious laughter rippled through Mayo. "By the way, with Hank out of commission, I need another man to watch my back . . . two'd be better."

"My, my. Have you misplaced your courage, Mayo?"

Between the grating voice and the slap against his character, Mayo's lip winged up into a sneer. "You want the cattle, you want the drovers dead, and you want the woman for yourself. With all them *wants,* I'd say you can spare the men. I'll take Smitty and Roy."

Another sinister laugh followed. "You amuse me, Mayo. Yes, you do." Then, in a gesture of dismissal, Humphrey said, "Smitty's the only one who can handle the cat. Take Pike and Roy. And just to show my generosity, you can have Chapman too."

Before Mayo departed, Humphrey clamped down on his shoulder. "If one hair on Dulcie Slaughter's head is harmed, I'll personally put a rope around your neck."

Mayo jerked free. Heat generated in his face. The threat didn't bode well. *Every dog has its day. Keep pushin', Humphrey. Keep pushin'.*

Chapter Eleven

Near Mossy Creek, the wind whipped up at the shale of the cliffs as though to scour them. Tiny grains of sand stung Donovan's face.

"What do you make of this weather, Teaspoon?" Donovan studied the darkening sky.

"Seen it like this once before, 'bout thirty years ago. Come a freak snowstorm smack-dab in the middle of July."

Donovan's ears picked up the drumming of horses hooves. He indicated with a nod. "Looks like Mayo made good on his promise to bring extra hands."

"Yep. But I don't recognize t'other three."

"Doesn't matter, as long as they put in a full day without complaint."

When the four riders pulled to a halt, Donovan's eyes shuttled to the new faces. Mayo hastened with the introductions. "This here is Pike, Roy, and Chapman. Mr. Humphrey wants Mrs. Slaughter to know that these men are on his payroll."

Donovan's mouth thinned. These were no ordinary cowmen. He'd stake his life the men Humphrey had sent were gunmen. The question was, why?

Donovan let loose a shrill whistle. He motioned for Toby and Sims to ride over. Sims' face gaped into a weird grin when he rode up and greeted the Rocking H hands. The reaction caused the short hairs on Donovan's neck to prickle.

"Teaspoon, Mrs. Slaughter all set?" Donovan's tone was terse.

"She is. Me and Toby helped finish loadin' the chuck wagon yestiddy. All's left is to hitch up the team."

Donovan sat motionless. "Toby, you're in charge of the remuda. Hold the string to the left-swing position about a half mile ahead of the chuck wagon."

"Yes, sir."

Donovan indicated the sturdy black mules still wearing their blinders and harness. He hadn't missed the salt rim caked around the leathers. "Tend your mules and then relay to Mrs. Slaughter we'll push out within the hour."

Toby gathered the lead rope. He twisted in the saddle to glance back at his trail boss. Donovan noted the boy's pinched frown. "If something's stuck in your craw, spit it out."

"No sense making animals stay harnessed all day, all night, and half the morning."

"Whatcha kick'n about, kid? They're just dumb, lop-eared jackasses."

Donovan's voice dripped with disdain toward the rawboned, harelipped man. "Chapman, you'll be first to ride drag."

Mayo cut his horse in front of Chapman's, blocking the way. "Donovan's the trail boss, Chapman. You'll follow orders or ride back to the Rockin' H and draw your pay."

The harelipped man scowled as he sucked against his teeth.

With a sharp sidelong glance, Donovan called out the remaining positions. "Mayo, you and Sims ride swing. Roy and Pike on flank. Except for the remuda, rotate your positions every second day. Teaspoon, you're in charge of Old Blue. You'll ride point all the way to Fort Apache. At night give Mrs. Slaughter a hand."

Chapman asked, "When do we switch wranglers for the remuda?"

"We don't."

The grim challenge written on the man's face verified Donovan's suspicions about him. The wind stirred upon

Donovan's neck, the grass around him bent, and the gray's mane streamed away. With the wind came a few large, scattered drops of rain.

"Teaspoon, get a rope on the lead steer." The gray horse shifted and pawed at the ground as if telling Donovan it was time to go. "Mayo, you and the men move the herd. Drive 'em hard for twenty or thirty miles until the steers are weary enough that the only thing they'll want to do is lie quiet for the night."

The gray moved out, wanting to run. Donovan pulled the brim of his hat lower on his forehead and let the gelding gallop toward the ranch.

Huddled in her rain slicker and wearing one of her husband's battered Stetsons, Dulcie waited patiently on the wagon's hard bench seat. She wondered what she'd gotten herself into. She'd wondered that quite a bit since coming to Arizona. It seemed that every adjustment she made, or considered making in her life, required another.

Still, the idea of several weeks on a cattle drive wasn't as much of a hardship as the life she'd left behind in New York.

She glanced up at the leaden skies and drizzling rain. She was all nerves and repressed anger as she thought back to the day she'd stepped off the stagecoach in Blountstown and was greeted by Jack Slaughter.

Always hopping out of the frying pan into the fire. How many times had she lived up to her father's disappointments?

Most of the anger at herself had faded. But the nerves were still there, jumping now as she considered what changes this trip would bring in her life.

The rain pelted the dry soil, lifting dust as it struck, bringing to the air a peculiar odor that comes when rain first strikes dry ground. The smell roiled Dulcie's stomach. *No, no, no,* she thought. She would not throw up the pitiful dry corn bread she'd choked down for breakfast.

Wishing for a strong pot of hot tea, she reached out to catch droplets of rain in her cupped hands and splashed the cool water over her face. She'd been suffering a great deal of morning queasiness, and this haunted her thoughts.

Worried by her feelings, she focused on the rider approaching the wagon. With such a formidable stature, he should have the face of a bare-knuckles fighter like she'd seen on posters.

He didn't. His was a striking face with a straight nose, deep-set blue eyes, and a pair of flat, muscular lips.

Donovan sidled the gelding close to the wagon. "You're looking a might pale, Mrs. Slaughter. Are you ill?"

She hastily brushed away her thoughts and squared her shoulders. She flushed. "I never get sick."

Although she'd never driven a team, she told herself she could do this. There was a moment of silence.

"This is my first cattle drive, Donovan. Shall I bring up the rear?"

"We'll push the cattle plenty hard to wear the edge of 'em by nightfall. Wouldn't want you in the way in case they take it in their fool heads to run.

"Once I pick a place to make camp, I'll fetch you forward. Afterward, you'll travel a mile or so ahead of the herd. That way, you won't choke on dust."

She swallowed and forced herself to meet his piercing blue eyes. "How will I know when or where to stop to prepare meals?"

Donovan's look brought a flush to her cheeks. She fastened a glare on him.

"I'll let you know, Mrs. Slaughter." He shifted in the saddle. Stretching his arm, he pointed toward the boy mounted atop a long-legged yellow dun. "Toby's in charge of the remuda. Keep him in sight."

A faint breeze danced up and swirled like music around the wagon. She looked at Donovan, breathless, as though the sight of a man wearing a wet slicker had cast a spell over her.

"Get them mules moving." Glancing up at the sky, Donovan pulled the collar closer around his neck. "I'll check on you from time to time." With that he set the impatient gelding toward the herd.

Feeling faint and sick, Dulcie forced herself to grip the reins and to sit straight on the wagon seat. Her voice was strong. "Get up there, Homer; you too, Plato."

She did as Toby had shown her and flapped the leather straps briskly across the mules' backs.

Getting the mules across the creek was a struggle. Dulcie's hands shook as she held tight to the leather leaders. What was it Toby had said? *Mules are stubborn cusses. Some will walk a mile just to bite a plug out of you.* He'd assured her that the matched pair of blacks was gentle as lambs—once she showed them who was boss.

Shifting the reins to one hand, she reached for the buggy whip, drew back, and flicked Homer's broad butt and then Plato's. The startled mules leaned into the traces, nearly jerking Dulcie from the seat.

She planted her feet against the footboard as the wagon splashed across the creek. She held the mules to a trot until she caught sight of Toby. Heeding Donovan's word, she kept a proper distance behind the remuda.

The miles fell behind and the storm swept westward across the vast reach to the mountains. Dulcie's arms ached, her back hurt, and her legs throbbed. Once again she had to confess that she'd stepped out on her own instead of thinking things through. Never mind. Whatever the consequences, she would face them.

"Mrs. Slaughter?"

It was nearly sundown and the rain had ended. The air was miraculously cool and washed clean and clear. Breathing it in was like a refreshing drink of water.

She turned quickly from her thoughts. Donovan was a hard man. An angry man. A bitter man. And he certainly didn't seem to like anyone standing up to him.

"What is it, Donovan?" Dulcie turned to face her new trail boss.

"Follow me."

And she did, to a grove of cottonwoods. When she pulled the mules to a halt, Donovan reached up and swept Dulcie from the seat. "We'll camp here for the night. How soon can you rustle up a meal?"

"Whoa, Donovan." Her head throbbed and her back ached. She forced herself to stop thinking of her Bible-thumping father, his demands and his belittlement of her. She placed her hands on her hips. "Let's set some ground rules. You don't tell me how to run the kitchen, and I won't tell you how to handle the men. And if you think you'll starve before I can get a meal prepared, then it's your own fault for not stopping sooner."

With her head held high and shoulders squared, she pivoted on her heel and strode to the rear of the wagon and unhitched the tailgate.

Teaspoon swung down out of the saddle and handed the reins to Toby. "I need somethin' for my rhemytism. These old bones of mine hurt in places I forgot I had." He stamped his feet as if trying to put some feeling back into his legs. He reached into his saddlebag and drew out a canteen. "Our secret." He drew a swig, coughed, and grimaced as the liquid slid down his throat. He winked at the boy, corked the canteen, and tucked it safely back inside the saddlebag.

Toby smiled and returned the wink before leading Teaspoon's horse to the tether line.

The old wrangler walked a bit stiff-legged toward the chuck wagon to help Dulcie throw together a quick supper.

Chapter Twelve

Slow drops from the leaves pattered on the canvas cover of the wagon. In the late dusk, the mountains were unnaturally green after the rain. Dulcie heard the creak of a saddle, Donovan's voice, and the low murmur of the men.

The melodic tune of a harmonica soothed her as she lay on her cot inside the chuck wagon. She drew the blankets high and looked up into the darkness. She didn't bother to stifle the yawn as her eyes fluttered shut.

Sometime later, she batted at the hands that shook her shoulders. "It's me, Miz Dulcie, Teaspoon."

She blinked several times trying to bring her eyes into focus. "What is it?"

"Don't mean to disturb you. Thought you'd like to know it's time to make breakfast. I already put the coffee on and some water to boil you a pot of tea."

"But it's still dark."

"Yes'm, if my old windup ticker is right, it's nigh on three o'clock. We best get to makin' biscuits. Trail boss is gonna want to pull out in 'bout two hours."

She bolted upright. "Start the bacon frying. I'll be out as soon as I'm dressed."

When the old man turned to leave, Dulcie caught him by the hand and whispered, "Thank you, Teaspoon. I promise this is the first and last time you'll have to wake me."

An hour later, she served up helpings of fried potatoes, thick strips of crisp salt pork, biscuits, and redeye gravy.

"I heard harmonica music last night. Who was playing?"

"That was me, Miss Dulcie. Hope I didn't disturb you." Toby offered a sheepish grin.

Dulcie placed an extra biscuit on Toby's plate. "Not at all. It was lovely."

When she handed Chapman his plate, he grabbed her by the wrist. "What about me, Missy? Don't I get an extra biscuit?" His fingers bit into her flesh as she tried to jerk from his iron grip. Chapman's harelipped grin added to the wickedness of his smile as he leered down at her.

Teaspoon rounded the wagon and pulled up short. "Git yer grubby paws off'n Miz Dulcie!"

Using the moment to her advantage, Dulcie drew back with her free hand and slapped the wrangler. Caught by surprise, Chapman loosed her wrist and in the process dropped his plate.

He growled, "Now look what you gone and done, missy." He reached over and grabbed a clean plate from the tailgate.

"Leave it." Teaspoon unholstered his pistol. "Trail boss ain't gonna take kindly when he hears 'bout this." With his old Patterson Colt aimed at Chapman's belly, Teaspoon said, "Ain't nothing wrong with the biscuit on the ground. Pick it up, brush it off, and hightail your sorry hide out to the herd."

"Aah, I was just funning. Cain't a feller have a little fun?"

"Mrs. Slaughter ain't no tildy-whirl gal. She's owner of this here outfit. You can save the fun for when we get the herd to Fort Apache."

Teaspoon gestured with the pistol. "Get now!"

With a disinterested shrug, the harelipped wrangler reached down and snatched the bread from the ground. He rubbed it against his shirt. As he chomped off a large bite, he winked at Dulcie and then swaggered toward the remuda to get his horse.

"I . . . oh dear." She shuddered. Her voice was a mere whisper.

"Toby, Teaspoon, please, let's not say anything about this to Donovan. He'll fire Chapman for sure, and we're shorthanded as is."

Teaspoon harrumphed as he holstered the pistol. "Man like him needs firing—maybe worse."

The look she gave him caused the old man to relent. He turned on his heel and said, "Mules are harnessed and ready, soon as you button up the wagon." He cast a glance at the boy. "C'mon Toby, time's a'wasting."

Dulcie's nervous laugh tinkled like a high silver bell.

The sun burned bright and hot. The smell of cattle and horses filled the air. Anger pushed at Chapman's insides. He resented riding drag and resented playing nursemaid to a bunch of long-horned brushpoppers.

He spurred his horse to ride alongside Mayo and searched the ridge line for signs of Donovan. "There's something familiar about the trail boss."

Mayo flapped the coiled lariat against his leg to keep the cattle moving. "You know Donovan?"

"Cain't rightly figger where I've seen him before."

"You ever go against him in a gunfight, mebbe?"

"Nah. He'd be dead if I had."

With a snort of irritation, Mayo said, "So other than havin' to ride drag, what's your beef with Donovan?"

Chapman chose to ignore the question. "I got a big hunger growin' inside me."

"Yeah, Mrs. Slaughter's a fine cook."

A steer broke from formation. Chapman spurred his horse after the black-and-white pied longhorn. A hundred yards later, he cut inward and hazed the ornery animal back to the herd. He resumed his position behind the beeves, his thoughts filled with Donovan and Dulcie Slaughter.

* * *

Dulcie had no idea the picture she made as she bent over the large frying pan filled with prairie hens that Donovan had brought her earlier in the day. A cobbler made from wild pears baked inside a Dutch oven.

She'd wondered about their food supply since leaving the ranch. In the months she'd lived at the Circle S, her husband never invited her to accompany him into town. He went alone, returning several days later and always with the excuse that his business was none of her concern.

With Teaspoon and Toby's help, she'd loaded the wagon with the meager larder: cured hams, baskets of potatoes, flour, a gallon jar of sugar, carrots, and onions. There hadn't been time for the garden she'd planted to produce.

Humming a lullaby, she used a long-handled fork to turn the pieces of chicken. She enjoyed this quiet time before the men filed in to heap their plates. It was tiring work, driving the wagon, loading and unloading the cookware, washing up the plates, and always having a pot of coffee ready for the men as they rotated their shifts riding nighthawk over the herd. All afternoon she had worked to put the evening meal together.

She pressed her hand to her stomach as emotions welled up and swamped her. Her secret was growing. Two weeks into the drive, and she'd already had to let the waistband out of her dress. Fiercely swiping at the tears building on her lashes, she refused to cry.

Her heart skipped several beats as a burly arm wrapped around her waist and roughly turned her against his chest. His stench caused her stomach to roil as she stared up at the yellow teeth grinning at her through a harelip. Pale and frightened, she nevertheless tried to keep her voice strong as she spoke to the man.

"Let me go, you filthy animal."

"Go ahead and struggle, missy. I like it when women fight."

Dulcie tried to free her arms. She lashed out with her foot, striking the top of his boot and causing no damage at all.

When his lips lowered to her throat, she huffed out an angry squeal. "I promise . . . you'll regret putting your hands on me!"

Toby fashioned a slipknot in the line he'd set, forming a makeshift rope corral. After stringing the tether line, he set to saddling fresh horses for the night shift.

When he heard the squeal, he wondered if Dulcie had burnt herself lifting a hot pot from the fire. Giving the buckskin a pat on the neck, Toby moved to the roan and lifted a saddle to its back.

The high-pitched shrill calling his name sent chills skittering down his spine. He scooted under the tether line and set his legs in motion, sprinting across the meadow. Adrenaline pumped through his body. His mind filled with thoughts of Dulcie catching the hem of her dress on fire, or worse, a rattler in camp.

It was a snake all right, the two-legged kind. From the distance, he couldn't identify the man forcing his attentions on Dulcie. He pushed his legs faster, losing his hat in the breeze.

"Let her go!" Toby grabbed Chapman from behind. His slight frame was no match for the man built like a brick building.

Maintaining his grip on Dulcie, Chapman flung the boy off. He laughed. "A pup come to save a she-cat." His laughter sounded like a snarl.

The boy went down without a sound, sprawling onto the grass.

"The fork, Toby. Get the fork." Dulcie had managed to free one of her hands. She clawed at Chapman's face. He backhanded her. She crumpled in his arms.

In one swift movement the boy grabbed the utensil, then rolled into a standing crouch.

Chapman whipped the .41 caliber Colt from its holster. "Ain't no skirt worth dying for, boy."

Holding the long fork like a weapon, Toby stepped forward.

Chapman taunted, "C'mon, pup. Show the lady what you're made of."

Dulcie's eyes fluttered open. She jerked rigid, her face filled with contempt. "Don't, Chapman! He's just a boy."

The next words were spoken low. "Pick on someone your own size, Chapman." In the heat of the turmoil, no one had noticed Donovan enter the camp until he stepped out of the shadows.

Chapman heard the words clearly. He shoved Dulcie aside. His pistol pointed at Donovan's broad chest.

Donovan looked at the hand gripping the Colt, then lifted cold eyes to Chapman's. "Only a coward shoots an unarmed man."

Teaspoon rode into camp. He pulled the shotgun from the saddle boot and shouted, "Leather it!"

With a swiftness that belied his stature, Donovan kicked the gun from Chapman's hand, then grabbed him by the shirt front. He smashed his right fist into Chapman's stomach, then shoved him backward and sledgehammered him in the face with both fists.

Chapman lunged, swinging. Donovan blocked Chapman's right and crossed over with his left fist. Chapman staggered and Donovan waded in, his face lined with fury. He hit Chapman with a left to the body, then a right.

Chapman backed up. Donovan slapped him. It was a powerful, brutal slap that jarred Chapman's heels and turned him half around. Then Donovan dropped him with a straight right—the bones in Chapman's nose cracking audibly.

Chapman sprawled on the ground facedown in the dirt. He rolled over, his body alive with hatred as he stared up at Donovan.

Pike hauled up on the reins and jumped from the saddle.

"What in tarnation's going on?" His hand reached toward his holster.

Teaspoon bellowed, "Wouldn't do it." He swung the shotgun toward the cowman.

Donovan's face was expressionless. "A man ought to pick better company to die with, Pike."

The rangy man lifted his hands away. His eyes darted from the old man with the shotgun leveled at him to Chapman lying in the dirt. "I got no quarrel with you, Trail Boss."

Donovan reached down and grabbed the gunman by the scruff of the neck, hauling him to a sitting position. "Take your boots off and get walking."

"What about my horse?"

"It's wearing a Rockin' H brand. I figure after Toby turns it loose, it'll find its way back to the ranch."

His voice thick with anger, Chapman tugged off his boots and tossed them aside. "You ain't heard the last of this."

"Then I'll keep listening."

Chapman gathered himself and shoved shakily to his feet. He used the tail of his shirt to wipe blood from his nose. "Next time I'll drop you where you stand."

"If there is a next time." Donovan motioned with his head.

Teaspoon prodded the gunman in the back with the shotgun. "Get walking, you jacklegged piece of vermin."

As Chapman pushed from the circle, he glanced back, and Dulcie caught the sneer. She knew his hate would harden into an evil thing.

Donovan watched the man go, his face somber. There was a small chance he'd run into Chapman again.

"You better put a slab of salt pork on that eye to draw down the swelling, Toby." A large bruise had spread across the boy's cheek, and his eye had swollen almost shut.

Dulcie roused from her stupor. She moved mechanically to

lift the fork from the dirt. Wiping the tines clean with her apron, she stabbed a piece of extra-crisp prairie chicken with a vengeance, slapping it on a plate.

Teaspoon walked over and sat a gentle hand on her arm. "I'll feed the men, Miz Dulcie. You go lie down, and I'll fetch a nice cup of tea to you in a bit."

She stared at him as if trying to comprehend what the old wrangler had said. She lifted a hand to her forehead. "Yes, of course. Thank you, Teaspoon."

Donovan watched her walk to the wagon. Restless, he grabbed a curry comb and brush. He went to his horse.

As Toby made a move to follow after Donovan, Teaspoon grabbed the boy's arm. "Leave him be, son."

He instructed the boy to scoop up a couple of plates, then he set about preparing a cup of tea for Dulcie. After he'd delivered it, along with a bowl of pear cobbler and an admonishment to eat, he walked back to the fire and poured two cups of coffee. From his secret canteen, he laced the coffee with whiskey.

He wandered over and joined Donovan. "Figgered you could use this."

" 'Preciate it."

"Don't you be careless, Donovan," Teaspoon advised. "That Chapman ain't likely to forget what you handed him tonight."

"Neither will I." He emptied the cup, handing it back to the old man. Running the curry brush over the gray's withers, he continued, "What do you know about Chapman?"

Teaspoon scrunched up his face. "Nothing. Only that Humphrey keeps a string of hired guns like him on payroll."

"What's Humphrey got that's so important?"

"Cain't rightly say—'cept living so far from town, and him being rich, it's likely he keeps a big payroll. Either that or he's afeared of the dark."

Donovan let the humor pass. He glanced toward the chuck wagon. "How's Mrs. Slaughter?"

"For a woman who's wearing the bustle wrong-sided, I'd say this little ordeal has mightily shook her up."

It was unnaturally quiet in the camp. There was no roistering or loud talk around the campfire. It even seemed that the cattle had settled in for the night.

"I don't catch your drift, Teaspoon."

"Why, Miz Dulcie's in the family way."

Stunned, Donovan stood for a moment, staring at the old man. Without a word, he turned stiffly, gathered the reins, and led the gray gelding toward the makeshift corral.

"Mayo, you out here?" Chapman understood the term *tenderfoot* from the ache in his bare feet.

"Chapman, where's your horse?" A cloud shifted across the moon, briefly lending enough light for Mayo to spot the man trudging toward him.

"He's a dead man." Chapman followed with a string of curse words as he detailed the fight with Donovan and how the old wrangler had backed Pike down with a shotgun.

Mayo sneered in disgust. "You couldn't bide your time, could you? Why, I ought to shoot you myself. Worse, we can't count on that beef-headed Sims to back us up."

"Then why did Humphrey send him along?"

"Clean the lard out of your brain. Humphrey wanted us to all act like wranglers. Sims is a bumbling fool. He's a mess-up that keeps the attention off us, you idiot."

As the seconds passed, tension grew.

Mayo snapped out his words. "Donovan's smart. He'll be askin' questions . . . might even take to watchin' me and Pike. How we gonna get word to Vesper and Smitty, huh? Answer me that, Chapman." Profanity spewed hot from his lips. "It'll be me answerin' to Humphrey if this operation doesn't go off without a hitch. And I won't take the fall for you because you couldn't keep your hands off the woman."

Chapman's own anger rose. "One thing's for damn sure, I ain't walking forty miles back to the ranch. Bottoms of my feet are already bruised, and I ain't climbing up to where Vesper and Smitty are camped. You're so smart, you think of something."

"Aw right. Shut your trap and let me think."

"Hurry it up. My feet's gettin' cold."

"Cattle are pretty calm, not much chance they'll stampede tonight. You ease on around and jump Sims. Knock him out and take his horse. Donovan will figure it was you. That'll take the heat off me and Pike.

"Hightail it to the ranch; send Waco back here. To keep Humphrey from asking questions, stay out of sight."

"Got any more suggestions?"

"Yeah, stick with Vesper and Smitty. After Humphrey pays Mrs. Slaughter a visit, it'll be time for the screamin' woman to haunt the mountains, mebbe even start a stampede."

Mayo lifted the revolver from his holster and handed it to Chapman. "Use the butt end to put Sims' lights out."

As Chapman turned to skirt behind the cattle, Mayo said, "Don't run off with my gun."

Chapman cut a sharp snarl toward Mayo. He stuck the pistol inside his waistband, then in a low crouch eased his way around the rear of the herd.

He reached up and grabbed the dozing Sims from the saddle. Before the startled man could react, Chapman crashed the butt end of the revolver against Sims' temple. He lowered the wrangler's limp body to the ground. Stepping into the saddle, Chapman rode to where Mayo waited.

"Walk out easylike, Chapman. No sense arousing suspicion by setting these beeves to bawling."

"When times comes for a showdown . . . Donovan's mine."

It seemed as if the night had swallowed the gunman. Minutes later, a low moan drew Mayo's attention.

Chapter Thirteen

The scent of tobacco tinged the night air. Pike rode toward the small red glow that winked like a beacon in the night. "Sims?"

"Nah. It's me, Mayo."

Pike pulled his gelding alongside the night rider. In a hushed voice, he briefly described the fight between Donovan and Chapman.

"Donovan sent him packing without his boots." Pike chuckled. "Never did like Chapman."

"Humphrey ain't gonna be too happy when Chapman hears he put his hands on the woman. You know how the boss feels about her." Mayo pinched the fire from the spent cigarette before flicking it to the ground. "Chapman thinks he knows Donovan. Just couldn't remember from where."

A loud moan drew their attention. Mayo said, "Reckon Sims is waking up. Chapman whacked him on the head and took his horse. I told Chapman to ride on back to the ranch, but he's not one to follow orders. My guess, he headed toward the hills where Vesper and Smitty are camped."

A weak voice called out, "Mayo?"

"Yeah, Sims, whadda you want?"

"Danged if somebody didn't clobber me on the head and stole my horse . . . took my gun too. You see who did it?"

Mayo kept his voice low. "Baby-sit these beeves, Pike. I'll act all innocent like when I ride Sims back to camp." He turned his horse. "Sims, stand where I can see you."

* * *

Dulcie removed a strip of rolled cloth from the medicine box. She soaked the material in cold water and then bound it around Sims' forehead, tying the ends in a knot.

"I'm afraid you'll have a headache for a few days."

Sims nodded his thanks and just sat there staring into the fire. "I always did figure Chapman for a low-down skunk."

Donovan handed the cowboy a cup of coffee laced with some of Teaspoon's special medicine. "Toby'll ride herd for a few days while your head heals, and Teaspoon will handle the remuda. You can ride in the wagon and help Mrs. Slaughter."

Sims held both hands to the sides of his head. He groaned. "Surely do 'preciate that, Donovan. Feels like a mountain fell on top of my head."

"We've had enough excitement for the night. Time to get back to work." Donovan turned to the boy. "I'll spell you in a couple of hours."

"Yes, sir." Toby gathered the reins, set his toe in the stirrup, and swung into the saddle. He merely nodded as he gigged the horse forward and rode out of camp.

Dulcie hugged herself and shivered, but her head was high and her shoulders squared. She started to say something but stopped herself.

Donovan approached her and laid a hand on her shoulder. "None of this is your fault, Mrs. Slaughter."

"I wasn't . . . I wasn't blaming myself."

"Maybe not out loud, but it's written on your face."

When she lightly touched his fingers with her own, he removed his hand as if she'd touched him with fire.

"Get some rest, Mrs. Slaughter. We'll push hard tomorrow. Breakfast . . . no nooning . . . supper."

When his storm-dark eyes pinpointed her midriff, Dulcie turned her face away to stare blindly out into the night. *He knows. Impossible. He couldn't.* Her mind warred with itself.

* * *

Through most of the night, Dulcie lay staring up in the dark at the canvas ceiling, following every sound she heard. She thought the morning was taking its sweet time about arriving. Although she was most shaken by her experience with Chapman, and then the attack on Sims, she felt safe knowing Donovan was near. A piercing scream iced through her already raw emotions and sent her scurrying from the wagon.

Donovan and Teaspoon stood back-to-back, each man with weapons drawn, slowly circling. Dulcie ran to them.

Sims scrambled from his resting place. "It's them. I heard it before—the spirits. I told you . . . didn't I tell you?"

The high-pitched scream sounded again. Dulcie trembled all over, shamefully torn between flinging her arms around Donovan or matching the bloodcurdling cries with her own.

The cattle's loud bawling jarred Donovan even more alert. His face darkened, refusing to give credence to Sims' superstitions. Even so, a prickling swept over Donovan's body. "Can't say I put much stock in ghosts and spirits, but whatever it is has spooked the herd. Teaspoon, you and Sims mount up. Mrs. Slaughter, get back in the wagon and stay there. And don't hesitate to use the rifle."

Sims, already in the saddle, said, "Don't matter if you shoot 'em or not, spirits don't die."

"Hold your tongue, Sims." Donovan barked orders. "Do like I say, Mrs. Slaughter. Get in the wagon, now."

Leading his roan and Donovan's gray, Teaspoon said, "Sakes alive, look yonder."

All heads turned toward where the old man pointed. Mesmerized, they watched three glowing red globes bounce across the ridgetops. Piercing wails rent the air followed by another and another.

Dulcie clung to Donovan's arm. "Dear god, it sounds as if someone is torturing a woman. And what are those lights?"

Donovan's hand went of its own accord to circle her waist.

He drew her protectively close. "There's not enough men to hold the cattle. Our immediate danger is a stampede." He placed his hand to the center of her back and gave a gentle shove. "Climb up on those boulders and stay there. If the cattle run, they'll smash the wagon into matchsticks."

"Be safe, Donovan—all of you." Knowing this was no time for an argument, she lifted her skirts and raced to the wagon, setting her toe to the wheel hub. She clambered inside and grabbed the rifle. Once on the ground, she reached between her legs to draw the hem of her skirt forward, tucking it inside her waistband to form a pair of bloomers. Then using a series of small boulders as steps, she awkwardly made her way to the top of the largest rock and settled high above the chuck wagon, with the rifle resting in her arms.

Breathing deeply and keeping her eyes trained for an ethereal enemy, she felt as if she wasn't real either but caught up in a bad dream she couldn't awaken from.

"Hold 'em in tight, boys." Donovan shouted, "Toby, whip out that harmonica of yours and play something soothing!"

Donovan worked back and forth, turning restless steers inward. He didn't have time for stray thoughts, yet his mind betrayed him and circled to Dulcie. He had no right thinking of her. She was a widow. It was his fault. The child she carried would be born without a father, and that too was his fault. He owned the deed to her ranch. He'd won it fair and square. His mind reeled as he felt himself pulled in many directions. Dismally, he realized there was no short way out of this mess.

His attention shifted to the sweet sounds of harmonica music lifted above the bawling beeves and then Toby singing "Get along Little Doggies," followed by more music. The boy had a maturity about him that almost made Donovan forget that at the tender age of sixteen, Toby was the youngest and least experienced of the crew.

Much to Donovan's relief, the cattle settled. Some lay down, while others milled. To keep from refueling their agitation, he cut a wide perimeter around the herd, speaking briefly to each drover.

"You all right, Toby?"

"Yes, sir."

"Good. There's still a few hours until dawn. Think you can play your harmonica that long?"

"Once, back in Pennsylvania, I played all night. Just need to wet my whistle ever so often."

"You have plenty of water in your canteen?"

"Yes, sir."

"Mighty pretty tune you played. Settled them ornery long-horns right down."

"Thank you, sir."

Donovan dipped his head and rode to where the old wrangler sat on his horse. "Teaspoon, ride on back to camp. Tell Mrs. Slaughter it's safe to climb down from the rocks. And you get some rest."

When the old cowhand pointed his horse toward camp, Donovan kept his voice even-toned. "Take Sims with you. If he falls out of the saddle, it might set the herd to runnin' again."

Donovan sidled the gray close and leaned in to Teaspoon, his voice barely a whisper. "I'm going on a little scouting trip. I need you to get the men and the herd moving, and keep them moving northeast until I return. Sims will ride in the wagon with Mrs. Slaughter. Still, I'll want you to keep a close watch for anything out of the ordinary."

"You going ghost huntin'?"

"My mother believed in spirits, my father in banshees. Real or not, I aim to find out what kind of creature we're dealing with."

"That was a woman if I ever did hear one." Teaspoon shivered. "Gave me the pure willies. Don't care if I never hear such a terrible thing again in my whole life."

"Switch mounts with me, Teaspoon." Donovan reached forward and patted the dappled gray's neck. "Human or phantom, can't exactly sneak up on it with the moon shining down on the General."

In the darkness, the treeless range rolled off gloomily on both sides of Donovan. He held the chestnut gelding at a slow pace to give it a breather and himself the time to set his ideas in order before gearing them into action.

With only moonlight to guide him, he crossed a flat at a quiet walk and approached a rounded hill shorn abruptly on one side, its flat face close against a smaller knoll. At the center of the path was total darkness. Donovan picketed the horse on a tough, gnarled bush growing along the side trail and loosened the cinch.

He rolled the cigarette in his lips, liking the taste of the tobacco, and squinted his eyes against the darkness. His black twill shirt, seasoned by sun, rain, and sweat, smelled stale and old.

An hour passed and there were no more screams or bouncing lights. He climbed up a crest where his eyes could just see over the ridge. Then he was hidden against a dark clump of juniper, where he was invisible to any eye not in the immediate vicinity.

The night was still and hot. Sweat trickled down his cheeks and down his body under the shirt. He studied the terrain with care, a searching study that began in the far distance and worked nearer and nearer, missing no rock, no clump of brush, no upthrust ledge. But he heard no sound, detected no movement.

He did not move. Patience was a price one paid for survival. Often the first to move was the first to die. He drew deep on the cigarette, returning his attention to his surroundings.

His eyes wandered along the ridge. To his right there was a shallow swale, the logical place to cross a ridge to avoid being skylined. Logical but obvious. His Comanche instinct told him the screams were real. Not human, but real. He searched his mind, recalling sounds made by his mother's people. Night calls of birds and mountain lions. No, a cougar didn't sound like a woman's screams.

He thought on this. It was something he knew, something born of years in wild country. Logic might explain the screams. But what about the mysterious red lights?

Finishing his smoke, he pinched it out and dropped it to the dirt and angled down the slope to where he'd tethered the gelding. He slid his Winchester from its scabbard, climbed up on a jutting lip, and settled against a boulder. He pulled the Stetson down over his eyes. Donovan could smell trouble and knew it was coming, for Mrs. Slaughter, the crew, the herd, and for himself.

Chapter Fourteen

Never in her life had Dulcie seen anything so forlorn, so unwelcoming, so dispiriting as the miles of mountain range that seemed to stretch on forever. She huffed out a breath and wished she could see its beauty. Unlike New York, there were no grand two-story houses. No pink-flowered curtains. No brick walkways.

Her spirits flagged as she stared off in the distance. It'd been two days. Where was Donovan?

A five-foot blacksnake slithered from under the wagon wheel and disappeared in a tuft of grass, eliciting a shriek from Dulcie.

"Don't worry about that feller, Mrs. Slaughter." Sims rounded the wagon in time to see Dulcie pale. "He's not poisonous. In fact, his kind keeps the rattlers away."

"Wonderful. How comforting." Dulcie peered over the Dutch oven while she stirred the beans. "What about bears and wolves?"

Sims settled on an upturned bucket. He lifted a potato from the pan and set to peeling it. "Wouldn't fret much about what you can see. It's what you can't that you need to worry about. Say, would you like it if I put your rifle where you can keep it handy?"

Dulcie shook her head. "I hate to admit it, Sims. I can cook and clean and can vegetables and make pickles, but mostly I'm all bluff. When it comes to shooting, I'm afraid I couldn't hit the broadside of a barn."

Sims picked up another potato. "Mebbe we should keep that little bit of information a secret. Sometimes all it takes is a good bluff to keep more'n just four-legged critters at bay."

Dulcie liked Sims and knew he was referring to the night Chapman had accosted her. Sims was a simple man with simple logic, and in his own bumbling way, his words offered comfort.

"It's been two days. Do you think something has happened to Donovan?" Her voice went quavery.

"No'm. He's a right savvy feller, that Donovan. I'd say he'll show up 'most any day now."

"What makes you think that?"

"'Cause unless I miss my mark, he's part Ind'an. That means it'd take a whole heap of trouble to put the kibosh on him. 'Sides, Donovan ain't a man who'd renege on anybody."

"In my heart I know you're right, Sims. It's just that he's been gone so long."

"How you want these taters cut, missus?"

With the way he'd skirted the answer to her question, Dulcie assumed it was Sims' way of saying the conversation about Donovan was over.

The afternoon was nearly gone when Dulcie set the huge coffeepot over the flat rocks atop the fire. Sims had gone to the stream to fetch two more buckets of water.

Only a few low tufts of cottony clouds floated in the wide sky. She was standing and looking toward the distance where Teaspoon was tending to the string of horses when something made her turn.

An Indian had come from the trees on the back of a gaunt brown and white pinto. She had heard no sound, no movement.

Another appeared and then another. Then they began to materialize from the trees as though by magic until there were six.

Their faces were flat-lipped and cruel. All the men were sinewy and dark-skinned and dusty. Their lank black hair hung to their shoulders, bound only with headbands.

One of the men sat astride a very striking paint pony. By his demeanor, Dulcie supposed he was the chief. Her eyes looked past him at a tall, evil-looking Apache who signed something to the older man.

Fear gnawed at her insides, bringing with it a sticky sweat all over her body. She forced herself to stand straight. Pale and frightened, she nevertheless managed to keep her voice strong.

"What is it you want?"

The tall Apache's flat black eyes made no change.

"I-I don't speak Indian. Do you speak English?"

The man stared at her, and the Indians waited.

"My men will come with guns if I scream."

The tall Indian, wearing three feathers tucked in his headband, slid from his pony. He spoke rapidly in the Apache tongue. He reached to touch her hair. She drew back and batted his hand away.

The warriors laughed.

He touched his pony's flaxen mane and said something, evidently comparing it to the color of her hair.

She did not scream. She couldn't. Nor would she allow them to see her fear. She fought back the rush of bile in her throat.

Turning down the valley, Donovan scouted around, searching for a sign, any signs of man or beast, but coming up with nothing. He started the chestnut gelding down the long valley at a steady trot.

He rubbed the scrabble of beard on his jaws. He rode on, remembering the woman stirring beans over an open fire and wondering how Dulcie had fared. She should have a man. It wasn't good for a woman to live alone. Nor a man.

And the child . . . it would need a father.

What kind of jasper would leave a woman alone fifty miles from nowhere, ride off to town, get into a poker game, and gamble away his ranch?

Jack Slaughter, Donovan reminded himself. The same man who'd planted three slugs into his chest and helped hang his brother and pa.

Still, it didn't answer the question as to why such a man would take a wife and then leave her alone.

From a high place in the mountains, Donovan's eye caught a glistening flash against the sun, and he reined up. His eyes were suddenly wide, and he grew angry. His thoughts leaped ahead.

Dulcie straightened her spine and raised her chin. She lifted her arm and pointed. The Apache wearing the three feathers in his hair followed her line of vision.

A horse was coming toward them at a dead run.

Dulcie shaded her eyes against the sun. *Donovan.* She felt her scalp tighten. The Indians seemed to have no fear.

Donovan slowed the gelding to a trot and rode easylike into camp. He unsnapped the trigger-guard from his holster before stepping down from the saddle. Standing beside Dulcie, his body touched hers. He made a sign to the Indian.

The Apache grunted. "I am Chief Three Feathers of the White Mountain Clan."

Dulcie huffed out, "I asked if you spoke English, and—"

"Be still, Mrs. Slaughter."

Dulcie clamped her jaw shut, heeding Donovan's warning.

"You are far from the reservation, *le mita cola.*" Donovan used the Apache words for "my friend."

"Strange things happen in mountains. Mr. Stiles, the Indian agent at Fort Apache, say he send cattle. We wait. None come. My people are hungry."

"What strange things happen in the mountains, Chief Three Feathers?" Donovan pressed the old man.

"Spirits weep. Nagi Tanka, the Great Spirit, is angry with white man who not respect Apache and our fathers before us. Our sacred burial grounds trampled on by men who bring their cattle. Now my people punished because we are old and no longer warriors able to fight."

"What else happens in the mountains besides the crying, Chief?" Dulcie asked quietly.

"Bloody souls rise from their graves and roam the mountains searching for those who disturb them, and bad things happens."

"No, no. Surely it's an asteroid of some sort." Dulcie held her place, hardly daring to breathe.

"Dulcie, he has no idea what you're talking about, and I'm not sure I do either." Donovan's tone was brusque, almost caustic.

The old Indian spoke again. "The spirits of our children cry out for food. You give cows."

It wasn't a question and Donovan knew it. He held up two fingers. "Mrs. Slaughter will trade you two steers."

Donovan saw the troubled look in Dulcie's eyes. "Point to something of his. Anything except his pony."

Dulcie bit down on her lower lip. She looked skeptical, but didn't press the matter. She pointed at the bear-clawed necklace. "I'll trade for that."

Chief Three Feathers removed the necklace from around his neck and handed it to Dulcie. "Good swap. Now you have powerful medicine against angry spirits, and my people will not cry themselves to sleep this night. We will feast."

Donovan glanced over to where Sims stood statue still, his hands gripping two bucket handles until his knuckles showed white.

"Sims, get your horse and ride out with the chief and his braves. Cut out two steers, and tell the men it's on Mrs. Slaughter's say."

The drover set the buckets down and untied his horse from

a tree. He looked a little more than worried when he followed the Indians out of camp.

Dulcie turned the necklace in her hand. "Why, it's not worth more than a few cents." She looked up at Donovan, her face pinched into a frown.

"It's worth more than you think, Mrs. Slaughter. By making the trade, you allowed the chief to save face in front of his warriors."

"Yes, but they were all too old to fight."

"They're hungry, not feeble. Another thing, Chief Three Feathers knows his people would be punished if he stole the cattle, which he would have risked had you refused to trade."

Dulcie's eyes rounded wide. "Oh."

"And the most important thing, Mrs. Slaughter, is you've made a loyal friend. The chief and his people will pay back that debt of friendship anytime you call on them." Donovan smiled at her.

She didn't know why she suddenly felt like a twittering schoolgirl. She just did. "Donovan, I'd like it very much if you'd call me Dulcie."

He stared at her for several moments. Rubbing his scruffy chin, he seemed to contemplate her request. "Yes, ma'am . . . Miz Dulcie."

She looked pleasantly impatient. She cocked her head to one side and studied him. "No, Donovan. Dulcie, just plain Dulcie."

Of late, it seemed being near the brawny man addlepated her. He was a man easy in his own skin, and just to be near him made her feel breathless and off balance. She had expected these emotions to pass while they were traveling with each other, especially since they disagreed about practically everything they had occasion to speak of.

Donovan's blue eyes lighted with amazed amusement and his mouth tilted upward in a grin. He reached out and tucked a wayward tendril behind her ear.

"What is this asteroid you mentioned to the chief?"

Her hands fluttered wide as if searching for a simple explanation. "They're like stars or small planets that . . . oh, never mind. It isn't important." Dulcie felt color rise to her cheeks when he gave her a bewildered gaze.

"I've seen shooting stars. My mother's people say they are lost spirits trying to find their way."

"Your mother's people?"

"My father was Irish, my mother Comanche."

"Was?"

"They are gone, for a long time now." Donovan's jawline clamped down hard. His expression changed from sadness to anger.

"Tell me about them." It surprised Dulcie how quickly he disguised his emotions behind eyes the color of a winter storm.

Donovan's large calloused hand gently gripped her chin as he drew her face to his. "Another time."

Dulcie closed her eyes, a soft breath escaping her parted lips.

"Apache!" The distraught cry caused Donovan and Dulcie to quickly regain control of their emotions.

Teaspoon galloped his horse into camp. Waving a shotgun in the air and shattering the magical moment between Dulcie and Donovan, he blustered, "Apache, they're riding toward the herd. C'mon, Donovan, grab your Winchester and let's get after 'em."

Dulcie laughed and held out the necklace she'd slipped around her neck. "It's okay, Teaspoon. Chief Three Feathers and I made a trade."

The old man eyeballed the necklace, a disgruntled look on his face. "I'd say you got the short end of the bargain, Miz Dulcie."

She lifted her nose and sniffed. "The beans . . . oh no, they're scorching. The lid, Donovan, hurry."

In all the excitement, she'd forgotten about supper. She scooped up a cup of water and poured it into the Dutch oven, sending a white vapor of steam into the air. The incident with the Apache was temporarily forgotten as she fussed over the pot.

Chapter Fifteen

A fortnight later, Clive Humphrey and two men cantered their horses down the old Superstition Trail leading toward Dulcie Slaughter's cow camp. She remained the sole owner of six hundred acres. He had an interest in owning the property.

It was unfortunate that Jack Slaughter had met with an untimely death at the hands of a gambler. Humphrey sucked back the grin tugging at his jowls. The gambler had unknowingly done him a favor.

Slaughter had outlived his usefulness. He gambled too much, drank too much, and it was only a matter of time before the liquor loosened his tongue and spilled out the secret they'd all guarded for more than fifteen years. With Slaughter out of the way, Humphrey intended to own the Circle S and Dulcie Slaughter too.

He'd met her just once and found in her a woman of impeccable speech and refined beauty, a slender, vibrant woman with a crown of Nordic golden hair. He'd never wanted to own anything as much as he desired Dulcie.

"You got a plan, Boss?" Frank Lowe interrupted Humphrey's musings.

"I do. I'll invite Mrs. Slaughter back to the Rocking H. By now, I'm certain she's longing for a proper toilet and something other than beans and bacon.

"With a kid, an old man, and a dunderhead for drovers, I'm equally certain the ramrod will appreciate two extra hands to help with the drive. That's where you and Garvey come in."

Frank Lowe patted the shooter at his side. "How soon you want us to scatter the herd?"

Humphrey chewed on the stogie. "No shooting, you idiot. You know how sound carries across these mountains. I'll not have anything rousing Mrs. Slaughter's curiosity."

It made no never mind to Humphrey that Lowe's lip winged up into a snarl.

"Garvey, you will volunteer to nighthawk—keep the cattle agitated. I don't care how you do it, just do it.

"Frank, you'll signal Vesper and Smitty to set the spirits loose. With all those bouncing red lights and screams, the herd will stampede, and then . . . Frank, it's all routine. By the time you, Garvey, Mayo, and Chapman plug holes in the drovers and six hundred head of cattle trample over them, anyone who happens along will think the poor, unlucky—" Humphrey let loose a phlegmy chuckle. He tossed the cigar away.

"Still didn't say how long you want us to wait." Lowe shifted in the saddle.

"Give me two days to escort Mrs. Slaughter to the ranch. I want her out of harm's way."

"What about this ramrod? What if he don't scare?"

"He'll scare all right. There isn't a man alive who isn't afraid when he's trying to turn a stampede."

Humphrey and his gunmen settled into an easy silence. He allowed his mind to wander as he planned his first meal with Dulcie. He envisioned her in a sunkist gown to match the color of her hair. He'd have the cook prepare quail and new potatoes with pearl onions and a corn soufflé and champagne; yes, he'd pop the cork on a bottle of his best.

The horse under him quivered and switched its tail. Humphrey swatted at a bothersome horsefly. He should have thought to bring the buggy for Dulcie's comfort. She was a lady, and a lady didn't straddle a horse.

For the first time in his life, he thought about an heir. A

newfound urge gripped him. He wanted a son. Dulcie was as healthy as a brood mare. She would give him a fine boy, of this he was certain.

The afternoon sunshine spilled like silvery fire on the waters of the creek. Donovan stood in the shadows, his shoulder propped against a tree, his arms crossed over his broad chest.

Dulcie sat on a rock with her bare feet dangling in the mountain brook. He thought her a vision of beauty.

"I saw a painting once of a woman staring out at the sea. Sitting there that way, you kind of remind me of her."

Dulcie released a startled gasp as she swiveled around, her eyes searching the tree line.

He stepped forward. "Didn't mean to startle you." Climbing on the rock, he sat beside her and removed his boots. "Water sure looks inviting. Mind if I join you?"

Dulcie rummaged up a smile. "It looks like you already have."

A short vibrant silence descended.

"I'm not usually a prying man, Dulcie. A body's private business is their own—"

"Whatever it is, Donovan, if it's within my means to answer, I will, but it comes with a price." She cocked her eyebrow; a grin teased the corners of her mouth.

"And the price is?"

"If I answer your questions, you'll answer mine."

"Sounds reasonable, and I'm a reasonable man. Most of the time." His eyes glittered down at her like shards of sapphire. He winked and gave her a lopsided grin.

"Are you teasing me, Donovan?"

"No, ma'am. Wouldn't think of it." He grinned roguishly.

"Then what is it you wish to know?"

"You're a woman of schooling and easy on the eyes too.

Why did you become a mail-order bride? Seems you could have had any man of your choosing."

She pushed from the rock and kicked the water, sending up a spray that dropped in glittering ripples on the creek's surface.

"I knew sooner or later the time would come when I'd have to defend my decision." Color stained her cheeks and temper flashed in her eyes. "My father was a teacher and a religious zealot, and in his eyes no one was perfect. When I was nine years old, my mother walked out of both our lives. We never knew where she went, nor did we ever hear from her again. Every day since, my father referred to me and all women as Jezebels.

"Nothing I ever did was good enough. And along the way, I made some wrong decisions. When my father developed consumption and there was no money to buy medicine, I made a bargain with the doctor to become his lady of pleasure in exchange for father's medical care."

Dulcie paced back and forth, her eyes cast down at her feet. "When it came time to . . . to . . . well, I couldn't go through with it. One of his proudest possessions was a statue of Rodin's *The Thinker*. When Dr. Haslett came at me, all I could see was an ugly, leering grin. I picked up the statue and hit him.

"I'm ashamed to say that I stole his wallet, and while he lay unconscious, I took several bottles of cough elixir too."

She felt ill, not to mention guilty. When Donovan didn't speak, she shrugged her shoulders and sighed.

"Fortunately, all Dr. Haslett suffered was a mild concussion. I was arrested and put in jail. My father visited once, to scorn me as a fallen woman. Then a friend, Betsy Winner, threatened to tell Dr. Haslett's wife the *real* truth if he didn't withdraw his complaint. She, that is, Betsy, is the one who showed me Jack Slaughter's advertisement for a mail-order bride. I wrote to him, and"—she spread her arms wide—"here I am."

Donovan stared at her for a long time. When he didn't speak, Dulcie said, "At the time, it seemed like a good solution. I'd have a home, food, protection. It seems all my life I've made decisions without thinking through the consequences." Her hands went protectively to her thickening waist, and though her sobs were silent, she couldn't still the tears. "And in a few months, I'll be raising the consequence of marrying a man I didn't know."

Donovan had slipped his boots on while Dulcie paced. "Did you love Jack Slaughter?"

It seemed an eternity passed before she answered. "He's the father of my child."

Donovan placed his large hands around Dulcie's waist and lifted her to the rock. He brushed wet sand from the soles of her feet. Collecting her boots from the ground, he longed to roll the long, black cotton stockings up her slender legs. Instead, he placed the boots on her lap. He looked intently into her eyes. "You didn't answer my question. Did you love Jack Slaughter?"

Before she had a chance to respond, a shrill whistle sounded, followed by an overly loud voice and exaggerated footfalls. "Donovan?"

It pricked Dulcie's pride to know that in some deep, wicked corner of her heart she resented the intrusion on this intimate moment.

"Over here, Toby," Donovan snapped.

The boy raced down the slope, his feet traveling faster than his body. He gasped, "Teaspoon says come quick. Three riders approaching."

"Any idea who they are?"

"Not yet. Too far away to tell."

"Help Mrs. Slaughter tote the buckets of water back to the wagon."

Donovan trotted up the hill, leaving her standing there

holding her boots. Dulcie let out a long, tremulous sigh to steady herself, but she felt hopelessly adrift.

Dulcie fashioned together a quick meal of fried potatoes and onions, corn dodgers, stewed dandelion greens seasoned with salt pork, and a pot of coffee. It was only proper to feed guests. She quickly unbound her hair, raked her fingers through the strands, and fashioned a neat chignon at the nape of her neck.

She shaded her eyes and watched the three riders stop to speak with one of the drovers. From the distance, she couldn't tell if it was Mayo or Pike. Perhaps it was Sims. He'd sworn his head was much better and he'd rather push cows than peel another potato.

She did recognize Donovan, his broad shoulders and the easy way he moved as if he and the horse were one.

They arrived a short time later. Clive Humphrey, his two hired guns, Donovan, and Teaspoon.

"I'll take care of the horses." Teaspoon gathered the reins and led the animals a short distance and hobbled them, then ambled on back to perch on a bucket.

Dulcie accepted Humphrey's extended hand. He placed his other hand possessively over hers. "Mrs. Slaughter, Jack was a dear friend. Too bad he was taken away before his time."

Dulcie discovered almost immediately that she did not like the rotund man with yellowing teeth and quavering jowls. She especially disliked the insolent way in which he looked over her without seeming to.

"I'm sorry, have we met?"

"Forgive me, my dear." He patted her hand. "Clive Humphrey at your service. I visited the Circle S shortly after your arrival. It was such a brief visit that it's understandable you wouldn't remember me."

She tried to remove her hand, but he held tight. "Of course."

This time she snatched her hand free and hid both in the folds of her apron. "What brings you to my cow camp?" She cut her eyes toward Donovan, whose face remained as wooden as a piece of mahogany.

"I've come to rescue you and to beg an apology for not offering to drive your stock to Kansas along with mine."

"I'm not quite certain I need rescuing, Mr. Humphrey. What is your intention?"

"Yes, well, a cattle drive is no place for a lady such as yourself." He turned toward the two men standing just behind him and motioned for them to step forward.

"Hank's hip is healing nicely, but he told me of your dilemma of working shorthanded. This here is Frank Lowe and Pete Garvey. Both top hands. They are at your service for as long as you need them."

She didn't like the appearance of either man. Both looked rawboned and mean. Dulcie said, "Thank you, Mr. Humphrey." She motioned toward the fire. "Would you and your men care to share a meal with us?"

"Mighty nice of you." Humphrey motioned for the men to sit. He lowered his hulk and accepted a plate, making an effort to touch her fingers. "It takes a talented cook to turn a meager fare into a delectable feast."

She wasn't experienced in the ways of men, but her womanly intuition told her this man wanted something from her, something she wasn't willing to give. "You didn't ride all the way out here to compliment me on my cooking, Mr. Humphrey."

"Quite astute of you, Dulcie . . . may I call you Dulcie?"

She didn't answer. There was something dangerous and barbaric about this man. She wondered if Donovan sensed it too.

She only knew what her senses told her and wondered why her hands suddenly felt so cold and clammy. Silently, she beseeched Donovan to speak on her behalf.

It was almost as if he'd read her mind.

"Mrs. Slaughter will do fine. It isn't proper to call a widow still in mourning by her given name."

Dulcie clamped down on the inside of her jaw to keep from smiling. She interposed smoothly before Donovan could say another word. "Did you come about business, Mr. Humphrey?"

Humphrey spoke with an edge underlying each overtly polite word. "No, Mrs. Slaughter. It's your personal character that I'm here to protect. People will not understand that you are a naïve young widow. Tongues will surely wag when a lone woman, without benefit of a husband, arrives in Fort Apache with men of questionable integrity."

Instead of flinching from this blunt observation, Dulcie looked Humphrey squarely in the eyes while he coolly continued.

"I've come to offer you the luxury of my home. There is no need for you to suffer the discomforts of heat and dust and insects. Not when I can provide you with a suite and a private bath. I, of course, will be at your disposal at all times. And I'm certain Mr. Griffin is capable of slinging together eatable trail food for the drovers. There is no need for you to continue to suffer this arduous journey."

Cutting his eyes to where Teaspoon sat on the bucket, Humphrey reached for Dulcie's hand and lifted it to his lips. "You are a handsome woman, Mrs. Slaughter. Perhaps in time, we shall become more than friends."

Listening to that rasping voice, Dulcie swallowed the nausea clawing at her throat. The look in Humphrey's eyes reminded her of a predatory animal stalking its prey. She sensed Donovan's demeanor stiffen and risked a hasty glance at him. Then, arming herself with a mixture of defiance and bravado, she smiled.

"I don't give two figs about my reputation, Mr. Humphrey." She smoothed her hands over her abdomen in a gentle caress.

She didn't miss the slight but veiled flinch in the fleshy rancher's eyes.

"In less than two months, I shall be in need of a doctor or most certainly a midwife. I will graciously accept your offer providing Teaspoon stays with me and that you send to Blountstown for a woman with midwifery skills, and who will act as my companion. And, of course, there is the possibility I'll need a wet nurse."

Unable to disguise his chagrin, Humphrey's jowls quavered. His hard mouth twisted into a travesty of a smile. "Well, to put it quite bluntly . . . hrrmm . . ." His voice seemed to hold a grim kind of humor. "I can see that what glitters isn't always gold."

Belying his hulk, Humphrey tramped to where his horse stood munching grass. He impatiently waited for Lowe and Garvey to remove the hobbles from their horses' legs. Without a backward glance, Humphrey and the gunmen spurred their mounts into a gallop.

Chapter Sixteen

Are you sure?" Mayo knocked back his work-worn hat. His eyes measured Lowe.

"Mm, yep. Sure as I'm sittin' here." Although Lowe had meant to speak in a whisper, his discovery caused his voice to carry louder than he'd intended.

Humphrey's voice held a certain alertness. "Why didn't you come forward with this before now?"

Lowe's lips twisted into a sneer. "I ain't got no crystal ball. How'm I s'pose to know who the woman had hired to trail boss her herd?"

Pike rode up and joined the group. "What's going on?"

There seemed to be a grudging twinkle in Humphrey's eyes when he said, "Frank was just telling us a bit of interesting news. Go ahead, Frank. Tell it again."

Humphrey felt a lightning jab of anger that Dulcie had not only refused his offer but had flung it back in his face with her announcement that she was carrying a child. Old scars had opened and his fury grew. He remembered another woman who had spurned him and had lived to regret it.

Lowe said, "The woman's trail boss is Ace Donovan."

Pike spoke up. "You mean Ace Donovan, the card shark?"

"Yep. The very same."

Humphrey growled his impatience. "Get on with it, Lowe."

A flush grew and spread along the gunman's scruffy jawline. "The night Slaughter was killed I was at the saloon in

109

Blountstown. Slaughter and Donovan were playing poker. The game was too hot for the others. They all folded.

"Slaughter was down to his last chip so he signed over the deed to the Circle S. Donovan asked him if he was sure that's what he wanted to bet. Slaughter threw the paper to the center of the table. Guess he didn't figure Donovan could beat a full house." Lowe harrumphed. "Donovan beat him with a royal flush."

"You're certain Donovan didn't see you?" Humphrey asked.

"Yep. After I'd finished my pleasure upstairs, I stayed at the railing watching the game. When it was done, Donovan knocked back the last of his whiskey, picked up his winnings, and left the saloon. Slaughter started rantin' about how Donovan had cheated him. He was like a bull seein' red. He stepped outside and shot Donovan in the back. Donovan hit the ground, rolled up on his knees with a Colt .45 in his hand, and put a slug right through Slaughter's black heart."

Humphrey shrugged in a careless fashion. He surmised that things had a way of working out. Dulcie had disappointed him, and he wanted to hurt her. Disappointment and revenge . . . they were synonymous. He would use Ace Donovan against her, and in the end he'd own the Circle S and the cattle. A low rumble built from his belly into a full laugh. He'd have it all.

Pike said, "Trail boss is comin'." All heads turned toward the dust kicking up around the hooves of Donovan's gray gelding.

Humphrey pulled out a bandanna and mopped his face. "Give me two days to get back to the ranch; then you men know what to do."

A zigzag of lightning cut across the sky followed by distant rolls of thunder. Donovan glanced upward as he rode toward where the men idled with Humphrey.

Something about the big-faced man created an itch inside Donovan's mind . . . an aggravating itch, the kind that scratching wouldn't relieve.

Outlying rumbles produced a maelstrom of activity among the cattle. Blowing and snorting drew his attention away from whatever was niggling at him.

"Vacation's over, boys. String out the herd." Donovan barked orders, letting his eyes rest on each man's face. "Lowe, you and Garvey ride flank. Pike, tell Sims the two of you are on swing. Teaspoon and I'll ride point."

Pike said, "What about drag, Boss?"

The sneer Humphrey cut toward Pike caused the hairs on Donovan's neck to prickle. A warning puckered the inside of his gut. "Put Roy on drag, unless Mr. Humphrey here is hanging around to lend a hand."

"It'll be night soon, Donovan. Only a foolish man pushes cattle in the dark."

With the sun dipping into the horizon, Donovan knew the risk of running the herd at night. "I'd rather risk the dark than endanger Mrs. Slaughter during a stampede."

Humphrey made no reply. With a bland scrutiny he hawked up a wad and spat on the hoof of Donovan's horse.

A roll of thunder broke the tension between the two men. Donovan bellowed, "Get those beeves strung out!" He glowered ferociously at Humphrey, then wheeled the gray about and raced toward the camp.

Teaspoon rode at a fast pace, his bony body leaning forward in the saddle. Donovan looked beyond the old man's shoulder. The chuck wagon was angling away from the herd. Donovan felt his throat swell with all the things he needed to say to Dulcie . . . all the things he needed to make right.

He pointed toward Teaspoon and then swung his arm to the west, pumping his elbow. The old man turned his horse, assuring he understood Donovan's signal to take the westward-point position.

* * *

An hour later, Donovan cantered alongside the chuck wagon. "How're you making out, Dulcie?"

"Is the danger of stampede over?"

"They'll settle for the rest of the night." Donovan moved to the mule and clasped the animal's harness. "Slack off on the leaders, Dulcie. I'll guide you to a spot where you can bed down till morning."

He tried to avoid thinking of her. The thought of her accusing eyes if she found out about him made him uncomfortable. He felt a rising anger and stifled it as he unhitched the mules and placed feed bags over their heads. The sound of their jaws grinding oats was pleasantly relaxing.

He rationalized that there was no reason for Dulcie to know about him or his past. He'd get her and the herd to Fort Apache. After settling the sale of the cattle and paying off the men, he'd give her the deed, explain how he'd come to shoot her husband. He had the document signed by the circuit judge explaining that he'd killed Slaughter in self-defense.

He was nothing to Dulcie and she was nothing to him. He was the hired hand, the trail boss. Nothing more.

Red balls winking on and off like beacons captured his attention. The piercing screams of a woman echoed across the mountain peaks, adding an edge to his thoughts. Fatigue and irritation mounted in Donovan as his eyes swept the darkness searching for the specter. He listened and the night listened around him.

The moon bled red. His mother's people called it a killing moon. The Comanche believed death waited for the morning.

There was a smell of damp and coolness in the air. Far over the mountains, low clouds gathered.

"Donovan?"

"Go to sleep, Dulcie. It's just the wind."

Chapter Seventeen

Lowe pushed his hat onto the back of his head, showing his receding hairline. Pete Garvey gave him a twist of a grin. Both men had followed Humphrey's orders to stay as far away from Donovan as possible until time for the showdown.

During their brief palaver three days ago, Humphrey had warned them. "Donovan is smart," he'd said. "Frank, don't give him any reason to suspect that you know who he really is."

Lowe's shirt felt sticky and uncomfortable. "Don't know 'bout you, Garvey, but I'm tired of eatin' a face full of dust. Humphrey's had plenty of time to get back to the Rockin' H, and I'm ready to call Donovan out."

"Yeah, and I'm ready to get to town and belly up to the bar for a cold one. You figured how we gonna play this?"

"Me and Mayo's been talkin'. We'll time it so that him and Roy, you and me will all end up in camp for noon chow."

"What about Pike?"

Lowe tsked. "Didn't figure you for a dunderhead, Garvey. Donovan ain't stupid. If we all show up, he'll smell a rat."

"Yeah, an hour from now we'll have him right where we want him." Garvey's eyes lit with a devilish grin. "We gonna string him up?"

Lowe patted the coiled lariat that rested against the saddle.

Dulcie sampled the spoonful of thick brown broth and determined that the stew needed more salt. The days had passed

113

quickly, each filled with its quota of work, but days that had her more and more often thinking of Fort Apache.

She rubbed the small of her back as she looked at the hills. The snowcapped peaks of the distant mountains reminded her of old men's beards, yet the hills were brown, the grass fading under the blazing August heat.

Strolling to the rear of the chuck wagon, she reached inside to draw out the small crock of salt and toted it to the bubbling pot. Using the wooden spoon, she lifted the hot lid, then counted out four pinches of seasoning and stirred.

She was lifting the biscuits out of the pan when she heard the rush of hooves and knew the men would come in shifts for the noon meal. Her heart thumped wildly when Lowe rode in first. She held reservations about Mayo, and except for Pike, didn't feel safe with Humphrey's men.

Lowe dismounted and dropped the reins. He walked forward and grabbed a plate from the chuck wagon's endgate. Dulcie rapped him across the wrist with the wooden spoon. He dropped the plate and yowled.

She spoke in a scathing tone. "Mr. Lowe, you will tether your horse away from the eating area."

"Are you loco, woman?" He looked mildly chagrined.

"I will not tolerate horse manure where I serve meals."

Lowe grinned. Dulcie backed away from his menacing step.

Despite her deep aversion to violence, she was hard put not to slap the cowhand's face.

Mayo rode in and swung out of the saddle. "Lowe."

The malice in Mayo's voice drew the gunman up. "Ah, I wasn't gonna do nothing. Just having a little sport, that's all."

"Horses don't belong in camp. Mrs. Slaughter's rules." Mayo offered Dulcie an apologetic glance.

Garvey dismounted and led their horses to the tether line a few yards from the camp area.

The men laughed, jostled each other, and swore happily. It seemed they'd made Sims the butt of their jokes.

By the time Donovan rode in, Humphrey's bunch sat around a makeshift table enjoying a game of poker.

"Hey, Trail Boss, we got an open seat. Join us." Mayo drawled the invitation.

"I'll pass."

Donovan accepted the plate of stew from Dulcie. She greeted him with the squeeze of her fingers. He tipped his hat and returned her smile. Finding a shady spot, he hunkered down on his haunches.

He watched the dealer cut the deck and then pass the cards around. Lowe gathered his pasteboards and fanned them out, ordering the cards. He peered over the edges at Donovan. The way Lowe's left eye ticked, Donovan figured the man either had a pat hand or was scheming to slicker his friends out of their money.

Lowe slapped the cards down on the table. He offered a wide-eyed grin at Donovan. "Say, it's just come to me where I know you. Fellers, this here is Ace Donovan, professional gambler."

Garvey picked up the rhetoric. "Nah, Lowe. You must be mistaken. Whoever heard of a professional gambler giving up the cards to trail boss a herd of mangy longhorns?" He cut his eyes toward Donovan. "Not unless he's on the run."

Mayo said, "You sure about this, Lowe? Could be a simple case of mistaken identity."

The gunman leaned forward. There was menace in his voice. "I ain't mistaken. He's Ace Donovan all right. I was in the Birdcage Saloon the night he cheated Jack Slaughter out of the deed to the Circle S."

A loud clatter and a little squeak drew their attention toward Dulcie. Her face had paled, and she hugged her middle. Her eyes shifted from the group of men to Donovan.

There was a catch in her voice when she said, "Is it true?"

"It isn't what it seems, Dulcie. I can explain." Donovan set his plate of food aside. Long days in the saddle and now sitting in a squat, his legs were slow to hoist his weight. Before he'd managed to stand to his full height, a loop settled over his broad chest, pinning his arms to his sides. He struggled to free himself. A powerful yank jerked him off his feet.

Roy planted a knee in the small of Donovan's spine. He used a pigging string to tie Donovan's hands behind his back. "Here he is, boys. All trussed up like a Thanksgiving turkey."

Mayo and Garvey gripped the butts of their Walker Colts. Garvey kicked Donovan in the side. "We're givin' the orders now, Trail Boss. Get up."

Mayo helped Garvey haul Donovan to his feet. Lowe swaggered forward. "Sorry to be the bearer of bad news, Miz Slaughter. Reckon you have a right to know that Donovan is the one who made you a widow." Lowe sucked on his teeth.

What was it he'd said that day at the creek? She squeezed her eyes shut. *I'm an honest man, Dulcie.* She managed to look at Donovan. "Why?"

Donovan struggled against the ropes. Garvey whipped the barrel of his Walker Colt against Donovan's cheekbone. "You were there, Lowe. Go ahead and tell her. The lady has a right to know all the details."

Lowe snatched the hat from his head and held it against his chest. "I'm sorry to be the one to tell you, Miz Slaughter." He recounted the night at the saloon and how he'd stood upstairs and witnessed the incident. "When Jack accused Donovan of dealing off the bottom of the deck, he challenged Jack to a gunfight." Lowe breathed out an exaggerated sigh. "Jack was dead before his gun cleared the holster."

"Dulcie—"

She held out her hand. "No, Donovan. I don't want to hear anything you have to say."

Mayo came to stand next to her. He offered her a cup of coffee. "You've had a shock, ma'am. Maybe this'll help."

She had not eaten since breakfast and yet she knew that one sip of the bitter, black brew would send her dashing for the bushes.

Lowe said, "Don't know how Donovan escaped the noose back in Blountstown, but I say let's string 'im up, right here, right now."

Donovan jerked away from his captor. "None of this is the truth. There's a signed affidavit in my saddlebag stating that I fired in self-defense."

Garvey went to Donovan's horse. He rummaged inside the saddlebag until he found the document rolled protectively inside an oilcloth.

Tossing the oilcloth aside, he unfolded the parchment. "Well, whadda you know."

Striding to the campfire, Garvey stumbled. His face lit with mock surprise as the affidavit fluttered into the fire. No one reacted when flames consumed the only evidence proving Donovan's innocence.

"Dulcie. The paper . . . it states the truth."

"What truth, Donovan? That you cheated my husband, stole our ranch, then murdered him?"

A ragged sob tore from her throat. "What kind of man does all of that and then pretends . . . ? You disgust me."

Lowe stared at Donovan. "Frontier law. Let's get on with it, boys."

Donovan lashed out and kicked Lowe in the groin. Dropping to his knees, the gunman spewed a string of cuss words. He gasped, "If we weren't going to hang you, I'd cut your heart out."

Fighting for his life, Donovan broke from Mayo and Roy's grip. He head-butted Garvey, knocking the man's feet out from under him. The gunman's face reddened from the ears inward.

Mayo tackled Donovan, driving him to the dirt and whipping the pistol butt across the back of Donovan's head, rendering him unconscious.

"Stop. Please!" Dulcie screamed. "Teaspoon . . . Toby!" She lifted her skirts to run.

Lowe caught her midstride and swung her hard against his chest. "Come now, Miz Slaughter. You're a grieving widow. You cain't go showing no loyalties to the likes of Ace Donovan."

He pinned her by the elbows, forcing her to watch Garvey fashion a noose out of the lariat. Mayo and Roy hauled Donovan to his knees while Garvey slipped the loop over his head and tightened the knot.

Faint with horror, Dulcie didn't know which man had yelled out, "Get a horse!"

Donovan shook the fog from his brain. He struggled against his captor's steel grip. With each struggle the noose tightened around his throat. He wasn't a man to beg or plead, but he refused to die without a fight.

Dulcie studied him closely, her face gradually glazing over with stoic expectation. He met her gaze, never flinching. She averted her eyes to the dirt, then forced them back up.

"I'm sorry, Dulcie. This isn't the way I'd planned it to end."

Her head dipped forward, her hair falling before her face. Donovan watched helplessly as the four men lifted him up on the horse's back. He swore at himself in silence. There was no sobbing. Instead an awful stillness gripped Dulcie.

Chapter Eighteen

Dulcie was swoon-headed with distress. She fervently prayed that Teaspoon or one of the other men would ride into camp for a cup of coffee. No matter her disgust toward Donovan, she didn't want to see him hanged.

It was the snuffle of a horse that made her realize they weren't alone. She hadn't heard the hoofbeats or the jingle of bridle fittings. Instead, she looked up and saw a tall man, with a lean, weather-beaten face and a distinctive snow-white moustache. He backed the authority in his voice with a 30-30 Winchester bucked up against his shoulder. "What goes on here?"

Lowe's irritation was obvious. "Don't know who you are, mister, but this ain't your business."

Holding the rifle firm against his shoulder, the stranger used his left hand to pull back his vest to reveal a badge. "I'm United States marshal Sam Cahill and I'm making it my business."

Garvey's hand edged toward his holster. Cahill swung the Winchester in his direction. "Wouldn't do it if I was you."

The marshal cut his eyes toward Dulcie. "You want to tell me what's going on, ma'am?"

"T-they said Donovan cheated my husband in a card game to get the deed to our ranch and then killed him."

Donovan lifted his head and stared at the lawman. Blood dripped from the cut on his cheek, his head throbbed, and he was certain the kick Garvey had rendered had fractured a rib.

"True, I killed Mrs. Slaughter's husband, but in self-defense."

119

Cahill said, "You got anybody to back your story?"

"I had an affidavit signed by the circuit judge out of Blountstown." Donovan nodded toward the smoldering embers. "Gone . . . there."

"One of you jaspers get this man off the horse. And get this noose off his neck. There'll be no frontier justice today."

When no one made a move, the marshal yelled, "Now!"

Donovan swung his leg over the saddle horn and landed on both feet. Mayo slid the noose over Donovan's head.

Donovan lifted the hands tied behind his back.

Cahill said, "Cut him loose."

Donovan rubbed the circulation back into his wrists. His face was drawn tight when he clipped off his account of the night. "The only proof I had is now ashes."

He was unsettled by the rush of feelings that swept over him. But he didn't let it last long.

The marshal said, "Too bad."

Mayo collected himself. "You didn't just happen by, Marshal. Maybe you're after Donovan here."

"Nope. Searching for my deputy. He was due back at Fort Apache 'bout two months ago."

Donovan's tone was cautious. "His name wouldn't happen to be Bert Nolan, would it?"

The unexpected announcement from Donovan brought a moment of silence. Marshal Cahill said, "You know Bert?"

"Met him about two months ago, shortly before I signed on with Mrs. Slaughter. I was unconscious when Deputy Nolan found me. The gunshot wound in my side had festered. He doctored it. Stayed with me until he was certain I'd live."

"Nolan say where he was bound?"

"Said after he investigated some suspicious goings-on here in the Superstitions that he was headed to Blountstown to pick up a prisoner, then back to Fort Apache. He didn't expect to be gone more than a week. And by the way, Nolan searched my gear. Once you find him, he'll testify to the affidavit clearing my name."

"Bert's a reliable man." Cahill made an irritated motion with his hand. "I'd like to think he's hurt and holed up somewhere healing. Little voice in my head says different." He turned to Dulcie. "Ma'am, I've got a schedule to keep. If it were me, I'd send these jaspers packing and without pay."

Lowe spoke through a bitter mouth. "What about Donovan? I witnessed him shoot Jack Slaughter."

The marshal pursed his lips. "Donovan, turn around and pull up your shirt."

Donovan darted looks between Dulcie, the gunmen, and Cahill. He did as he was told and turned around and pulled the tail of his shirt from the waistband and lifted it high. He slowly rotated to face the lawman.

Dulcie bit her lip to keep from crying out. Several old scars marked his chest and shoulders and gave clear evidence that this was a man who had frequently faced the challenge of his enemies and had lived to speak of it.

She stood there staring at a raw-puckered scar. The entry wound to Donovan's back was small, but where it had exited in the front and below his heart had left an indentation the size of her diminutive fist.

The marshal's eyes flashed with disgust. "I hold more respect for a rabid wolf than I do for a backshooter."

The horse under him shifted, and Cahill said, "Think I'll ride on to Blountstown to see if Bert took delivery of the prisoner."

Donovan tucked the tail of his shirt inside his waistband. "You know sheriff Tom Horn, Marshal?"

"Him and me have swapped a few lies in our lifetime."

"Ask him about the night I shot Jack Slaughter. He'll remember."

Cahill chuckled. "That old coot has a memory like an

elephant." He cradled the Winchester in the crook of his arm and leaned forward, his eyes focused on Lowe and Garvey. "Think I'll shuffle through my stack of wanted posters when I get back to Fort Apache. 'Pears I've seen your faces somewhere."

He touched the brim of his hat and turned his horse from camp.

Teaspoon wore a puzzled frown when he swung out of the saddle. "I just seen a stranger ride out of camp and then two of Humphrey's men hightailing it yonder." He pointed to a receding cloud of dust. "And Mayo was with 'em . . . what the dickens happened to you?"

Donovan sat on a bucket while Dulcie bound his ribs with a roll of cloth. He looked up sharply. "The man on the sorrel was marshal Sam Cahill. His deputy is overdue bringing in a prisoner . . . thinks he may have come to a bad end. Too bad. Bert Nolan struck me as a decent sort."

Dulcie tightened the knot, causing Donovan to suck in a painful breath. He sat hunched over; pain was beginning to work on him and when he spoke there was a tightness in his voice to betray it.

Teaspoon helped himself to a plate of stew. He pulled a bucket around and straddled it. His expression was bleak as he listened to Dulcie's explanation of what had transpired.

He jammed a spoonful of beef into his mouth and chewed furiously. He gestured with his spoon, poking the air in front of him. "Nothing but a bunch of yellow-bellied sapsuckers. I knowed it all the time."

Dulcie's thoughts whirled. She felt as if a dense cloud had hung over her for a long, long time. She stepped away from Donovan. She knew she had no right to feel betrayed, but she did. She felt betrayed by fate for putting her in this position at the precise time she'd let down her guard with Donovan. She watched the pain darken his eyes.

"We're three men short. What will we do now, Donovan?"

His jaw tightening visibly, he looked at her as she stood before him, studying him pensively.

Dulcie stared at him outright. She had to give him credit. He didn't shy away from admitting he killed her husband, at least not today. And he'd done so with such a fine dignity that she couldn't help but be stirred by the burden that rested upon his shoulders of seeing her and the cattle safely through to Fort Apache.

"I-I'd appreciate it if you would stay."

"If you're sure . . . ?"

She was anything but sure. "It's strictly business, of course."

He merely answered with that signature unruffled look of his from beneath the battered brim of his tan Stetson.

Dulcie blinked rapidly. She didn't know what showed on her face, but whatever it was seemed to compel Donovan to reach out and touch her.

Her stomach flip-flopped and then pain sliced through her midsection as sharp as any knife. She felt herself sliding into darkness.

Chapter Nineteen

Dulcie rested inside the wagon. She worried her bottom lip with her teeth while listening to Donovan's voice, pitched low, filter through the canvas.

"What do you think, Teaspoon? Too much anxiety for Dulcie?"

The old wrangler answered in a low rumble. "Dagnabit, Donovan, if I don't miss my guess, I'm thinkin' Miz Dulcie's miscalculated her time."

Dulcie shifted to a more comfortable position. She searched her memory for the last time her menses had visited. Was Teaspoon right? Had she miscounted? What she did know was how unsettled she felt miles from nowhere and miles from a doctor.

She imagined Teaspoon, sometimes crotchety and even surly at other times, pacing back and forth, his leathery face scrunched into a frown.

She blanched at Donovan's comment. "Dulcie's a brave but foolish woman. You think her time is closer than she knows?"

"If'n she was a mare, I could tell you. But consarn it, she ain't."

Arizona was experiencing what seemed to be a spell of Indian summer. Even though the sun had set, the temperature remained uncomfortably hot, leaving the interior of the wagon muggy and close.

Dulcie buttoned the bodice of her dress and wiped the moisture from her cheeks. Ten minutes later she stepped down from the wagon and confronted both men with a stalwart gaze.

124

"I'll admit that I am more than a little concerned the baby will decide to come before we get to a doctor. Do either of you know a shortcut to Fort Apache?" She wrapped her arms around her middle. "I'm willing to lose a few head of cattle if need be."

She still harbored bitterness toward Donovan and was quite certain nothing he could say or do would change her feelings. He looked thoroughly disreputable and thoroughly dangerous. But right now she needed to trust him.

Donovan gave an exaggerated sigh of exasperation before he sauntered toward her with a jingle of spurs. "If you'll excuse my familiarity, Mrs. Slaughter, I don't think you'll last another three weeks, much less the rigors of crossing an uncharted trail that might add days instead of shortening them." He shoved the Stetson back on his head.

So it had come to that—"Mrs. Slaughter" again. She had said "strictly business," hadn't she?

Donovan sounded matter-of-fact as he explained his plan. "We'll use the extra canvas to set up a makeshift kitchen for Teaspoon. I'll double team the mules with two horses. With the extra pulling power and a lightened load, we ought to make Fort Apache in ten days. Be ready to pull out at dawn, Mrs. Slaughter."

He shifted his attention to the old wrangler. "Teaspoon, there's enough graze and water to last until I return. Once I see the boss-lady settled, I'll ride back with a crew to help bring in the herd."

Dulcie's heart was tight and cold within her when she bade the men good night.

Donovan's body ached from the beating he'd received from Humphrey's saddle tramps. He turned up the cup and swallowed the last drop of coffee laced with a generous dose of Teaspoon's medicinal elixir. Propped against his saddle, he studied the terrain with care, a searching study that began in the far distance and worked nearer and nearer to the camp. He saw no dust, heard no sound except the stirring of cattle, detected no unusual movement. His eyes wandered along the ridge. Every instinct told him trouble was coming. He eased his length down on his bedroll to a more comfortable position and sifted through his memory; the name Humphrey stood out.

Donovan resisted the exhaustion tugging at him until his face relaxed and sleep crowded in on him. Ghostly images floated behind his eyes . . . images of his father and brother, hands tied behind their backs . . . a raspy voice yelling, "Hang these farmers!"

Laughter echoed inside Donovan's mind. A phlegmy laughter. And he saw himself, seventeen years old and bleeding from multiple gunshot wounds. Another voice came to him, that of Jack Slaughter saying, "C'mon, Humfried, we did what we were paid to do. Let's make tracks before someone spots the fire."

A bear of a man hawked and spat a wad of foul mucus.

Donovan stirred in his sleep. He seemed to feel the wetness and reached up to wipe his forehead. Realization came in small clicks. Donovan knew Humfried and Humphrey were one and the same—the faceless man from his past.

His stomach twisted as it had that night he'd witnessed Humphrey and his night riders burn his family home and barn, run off all the livestock, and leave him for dead.

The hard ground fretted his bruised body. He shifted, seeking a more comfortable position. On the fringes of consciousness, Donovan struggled to untangle his thoughts.

In the distance, a woman's scream echoed and then died. It was as if the night held its breath and the moon was a blemish behind the clouds.

Drenched in sweat, Donovan sat up. He gazed at his hands,

which were trembling. He heard the cattle, the horses, and the shooting, a directionless uproar that seemed to come from the sky. The ground beneath him vibrated.

The cracking of gunfire brought him to his knees. The firing was a stunning noise against the backs of the stampeding herd. Donovan counted them—seven horsemen. Featureless figures in the dark.

Seven of them. What kind of raid is this? And then he knew. Beyond the wild yells, he recognized Frank Lowe's voice shouting to the others to keep firing, to run the cattle straight through the camp.

The mules began to bray wildly and reared against their tethers. A slug tore into the neck of one of the mules. It screamed in pain and keeled to one side.

Someone bawled, "Whar's Ol' Blue? Gotta turn the herd."

Bullets sang past as Donovan dashed for the chuck wagon. His only concern was Dulcie's safety.

With Colt .45 in hand, he triggered three shots in fast succession at the frenzied herd. He swept a gaze past the wagon to where the trunks of three Palo Verde trees stood lodged together, creating a crevasse large enough to squeeze a small body inside.

"Dulcie, get out of the wagon. Now!"

She stood on the wheel and stretched out to him. He reached up and swept her into his arms.

"The baby . . . I'm afraid, Donovan."

"It'll be all right. Don't worry."

The stand of Palo Verde stood still and quiet. Donovan's eyes had adjusted to the darkness to differentiate between the shadows and the thick bole of the trees. Setting Dulcie on her feet, he instructed her to wedge in between the trunks that provided a makeshift fortress.

"Whatever you do, Dulcie, don't panic. The cattle and horses will surge around the tree's thick base. You'll be safe." He admonished her, "Tear off a strip of your skirt and tie it around your mouth and nose to keep from choking on the dust."

There was a look of profound terror in Dulcie's eyes. "What about you?"

His face drawn tight and stony, Donovan cautioned her, "Don't leave the trees until Teaspoon or I come for you."

"But what . . . what if you don't?"

He touched her hand to the side of his face and held it there lightly for a mere moment, then walked away without looking back. Morbidly it occurred to him that he might not live to see another sunrise. The blood of his mother's people sang through his veins. It was a good day to die.

He checked the chambers of his pistol. His stomach twisted as it had the night Humphrey and Slaughter had hanged his father and brother.

He raced forward.

A shot bounced with a reverberating boom above the din of thundering hooves. With the animals bawling and the riders wheeling them into a mass of confusion, Donovan halted and aimed. He fired twice. A horse reared and the rider disappeared in the tangle of longhorns.

The calling of his name spun him around, his gun poised, searching the shadows. He swiveled on his heels and raised his Colt.

"You're a dead man, Donovan."

"Yeah, who says?"

"You broke my nose."

"Chapman?"

The short hairs on Donovan's neck prickled. A noose settled over his broad shoulders. He worked one arm free before the loop tightened. His feet were jerked from beneath him as a second rope wrapped around his chest. He crumpled into an awkward twist as he hit the ground. Before he could react, a horse lunged forward. Reaching up to grab the rope with his left hand, Donovan's right arm remained trapped against his body.

Frank Lowe bellied out a laugh. "We got 'im now, Chapman. Let's take him for a ride he'll never forget."

The horses squealed and raced into a full gallop. Donovan tried to relax as his body was dragged across patches of thorny cacti. His shoulder brushed against a piñon tree. He felt the fabric of his shirt shred away, leaving his chest exposed. Dirt acted as sandpaper against his skin.

The hot breath of cattle and their deafening thunder closed in around him. If dragging him to death didn't work, the gunmen meant to make it look as if his horse had gone down in the stampede, leaving Donovan trampled beyond recognition.

In the darkness, the range rolled off gloomily on all sides of him. Voices and pistol fire vibrated inside his head. His jackknifed legs ached and his lungs seared as he bounced inches ahead of the stampede. Donovan's head collided with a boulder, and he felt the energy running out of him. The ropes went slack.

Horses' hooves drummed past a mound off to the side of a dip in the land. Donovan rolled into a hollow and pulled himself into a tight ball. Through a red haze of pain, he spied a cluster of boulders. Trying to get to his feet, his legs let him down. He snaked on his knees and elbows across the short distance, wedged between the rocks. Inside his head, he sang the death chant of his mother's people.

Chapter Twenty

In spite of the early dawn that powdered the sky with a pink and gray haze, perspiration pooled between Donovan's shoulder blades.

He fought against the cramped deadness of his limbs. He wriggled from between the rocks, got to his hands and knees and pushed to both feet. He used a hand to steady himself.

A profound tiredness gripped him. He lowered his body against the boulder. A muscle in his jaw tightened as he surveyed the mangled land. Off in the distance, the chuck wagon lay splintered like cordwood. For a few minutes nothing stirred.

Despite himself, he let his mind drift. He was deep in thought when padded steps halted behind him. Numb with exhaustion, Donovan didn't look up until he heard the soft nicker and felt a gentle nudge against his shoulder. "General, you old sonafagun! Am I ever glad to see you."

He reached around and clasped the dangling reins, then leaned his head against the gray gelding's neck.

The sun was mostly huddled behind the mountains. Somewhere in the distance a bird chirped. The landscape was a sobbing blur to Dulcie as she removed the strip of cloth from around her nose and mouth to inhale the morning freshness.

She was frightened and tried not to admit it to herself. All through the night she had felt a change at work within her body. Her time was near.

"You've been restless all night, baby," she said aloud as the

130

child nestled inside her womb moved. "Be patient a little longer, baby. Please don't come. Not yet." She tried to drive the worry from her mind.

Recalling Donovan's words to not leave her den of safety until he or Teaspoon came for her, she brushed the heaviness from her eyes and surveyed her surroundings.

A cold horror shook her as the scene in front of her unfolded. The land looked as if a violent storm had broken and twisted everything in its path.

A few head of cattle straggled about. A horse thrashed and screamed in pain as it struggled to stand; its front leg dangled at an awkward angle.

Dulcie ran her tongue over her parched lips. A strong kick to her middle caused her to huff out a breath. She caressed her stomach as if reassuring her unborn child that it was safe.

The vastness of the land loomed in front of her, sinister and gloomy. As the pain in her abdomen increased, her hands tightened into fists. In spite of Donovan's admonition to stay put, she eased herself from the tree's crevasse and into the open. Testing her cramped legs, she stood, trembling. Where were Donovan and Teaspoon? And what about Toby? How would she ever face a sixteen-year-old boy's parents to tell them their son had died? That and the fact that she might be all alone made her physically ill.

Like undertakers in black suits, buzzards swooped down from the sky and squatted. In the many months along the trail, she'd seen how vultures had flocked around animals, waiting for them to die—sometimes pecking at the poor miserable creatures only to increase their misery. The horse with the broken leg lost its balance and fell and the vultures moved in on the prey.

Something inside Dulcie broke. She forgot about the pain slicing down the small of her back. Anger drove her to load both of her fists with rocks, and with brisk strides, she marched toward the wild-eyed, defenseless horse and began chucking rocks at the buzzards. When her hands were empty, she bent down and gathered clods of dirt to throw.

As the carrion eaters rose and soared and settled again, she flailed her arms and screamed, "Hades! Get out of here! Shoo! Be off with you!"

She waded through the birds, kicking their sinister bodies and watching them scatter and then settle again at a safe distance. With the awkwardness of a woman in late trimester, Dulcie sat next to the horse and lifted its head into her lap.

"It's okay, horse. Donovan will come for us. He promised."

She stroked the gelding's neck, crooned to it, and listened to the animal's labored breathing.

In the hot stillness of the morning, Donovan spotted her sitting with the horse. A mixture of anger and relief surged through him. Angry because she hadn't stayed at the Palo Verde tree as he'd instructed. Relieved to find her alive.

The image she and the horse created against the backdrop of a pale blue sky filled with billowing clouds struck him as ethereal, but he had too much on his mind to admire the scenery.

All too familiar with the danger the injured animal posed to Dulcie, Donovan circled his gray gelding in a wide swath to ride up behind her.

He stepped out of the saddle and dropped the reins, knowing the horse would stand ground-tied. Donovan stole softly to her side. He spoke in a quiet, calm voice. "Dulcie, are you all right?"

"He has a broken leg."

From the dry, even crispness in her voice, Donovan figured she was in shock. "Can you move away from him?"

She shook her head. "I don't think so."

"How long have you been like this?"

The gelding grunted, lifted its head, and rolled its eyes toward Donovan.

Dulcie sniffed. Her shoulders moved up and down with the long sigh. She stroked the injured animal's cheek. "It seems forever."

"He's hurt. That makes him dangerous."

"I know."

"I'm going to ease you out from under him and lift you away."

"No. You'll shoot him."

"He's suffering, Dulcie."

She nodded her understanding.

Donovan moved within an inch of Dulcie. He gently touched her shoulder before reaching under her arms. He felt her stiffen and knew he had to act quickly before her unease transferred to the injured gelding.

He swallowed the knot in his throat and sucked in a deep breath. His tall frame slightly bent, his eyes alert, his shoulders rigid, and his mouth drawn in a tight line, he wrapped his arms securely around her trembling form. He called upon all the strength in his exhausted and ravaged body to lift Dulcie. He skittered backward away from the horse, Dulcie's heels dragging in the dirt.

A safe distance from the thrashing animal, Donovan scooped Dulcie into his arms and carried her to where the gray gelding stood munching grass. Setting Dulcie on her feet, he pulled the Winchester from the rifle scabbard.

"Please," she pleaded, her eyes brimmed with tears.

Donovan slapped his thigh in exasperation. He spun on his heel and booted the rifle against his shoulder. The explosion of gunfire resounded, echoing over the mountains, scattering the buzzards from their resting place and penetrating the stillness.

Dulcie cast him a damning look. She wore a mask of pain,

anguish, and fury. She raised both fists and pummeled his raw and bleeding chest.

Donovan stood there, allowing Dulcie to batter his chest. She was a little thing but had gotten so big with the baby she looked like she might topple over from the weight. When her breathing became labored, he clasped his work-calloused hands around her wrists.

With a murmured curse, Donovan said, "Enough, Dulcie."

Stepping back from him, she dashed at her eyes with the back of one hand and still the tears came. Her chin trembled as she spotted the blood staining through his clean shirt.

"I've hurt you . . . I-I'm . . ."

She reached for him, and he brushed her hand aside. "You didn't do it."

"Were you shot?" Concern puckered Dulcie's brow.

"Frank Lowe and Chapman dragged me." He harrumphed. "Won't they be surprised when they find out I'm not dead."

Dulcie opened her mouth to say something, but instead she cried out in pain. He watched the color drain from her face, a sense of dread weighing down his spirit.

By midmorning the sun had burned through the haze and settled its warmth upon the prairie. Donovan held Dulcie in his arms while holding the gelding at an even gait. He watched the shifting patterns of the clouds. A bump against his elbow pulled him from his introspection.

"What was that?"

He felt her smile in the sigh. "The baby just kicked."

Panic stitched through him. "It's not time . . . I mean . . . you're not . . ."

"Not yet, but soon, I'm thinking."

"Has the pain eased?"

She rested her head against his chest. He heard the tiredness in the way her voice cracked. "I'm worried about Teaspoon and Toby."

"The aftermath of every storm is tranquility."

"What?" Dulcie shifted to look up at Donovan.

He smiled. "It's something my mother used to say."

"Tell me about your mother."

When he didn't answer, Dulcie prompted, "It'll take my mind off . . . things."

Afraid of jarring Dulcie and adding to her discomfort, Donovan longed to gig the gelding to a faster pace. He scanned the horizon for signs of the old wrangler and young boy. His Comanche instinct told him another storm was coming, and he needed to find a safe place for Dulcie.

"My mother's name was Shell Woman. She was Comanche. Her husband had been killed in a battle with the Sioux. The Sioux took my mother prisoner and made her a slave. My father was an Irishman who traded with the Lakota. He fancied my mother and paid four ponies and a skinning knife for her."

Dulcie relaxed, and he tightened his arms around her.

"Shell Woman. Was your mother as beautiful as her name?"

Even now he recalled the gentle doe eyes, the hair the color of shiny black plums, and the laughter in his mother's voice when she'd scold him and his brother. Thoughts of her brought a strange, bittersweet poignancy.

"Yes, she was." His voice was quiet.

He scanned the surrounding countryside, as though he expected Humphrey's men to return.

"Where are we going, Donovan?"

In an effort to put her mind at ease, he discarded the option of a ten-day ride to Fort Apache. The gelding beneath him was strong and had carried him far, but never with double the load.

"There's not much left of the chuck wagon. Maybe I can salvage the canvas. As soon as I rig up a shelter for you, I'll build a fire and signal Chief Three Feathers."

He didn't have to wait. A flurry of dust in the western horizon drifted toward him. He hauled up the gelding.

Dulcie roused forward. "What is it?"

"Riders." He pointed.

"Teaspoon?"

"From the dust they're kickin' up, I'd say it's more than one or two heading this way."

"Not Lowe and the others?" She shuddered and pressed against him. "Would they be coming back for the spoils?"

Donovan lifted the revolver from its holster. "Hide this in the folds of your skirt." He reached for the Winchester and pulled it from the rifle boot, his finger resting on the trigger. "If it is them, don't fire until they're a hair's breath from us."

"Donovan . . . Miz Dulcie, danged if I ain't proud as a peacock to see you."

Dulcie released a long, shuddering sigh. Relief coursed through her at the sight of the old wrangler. "Your arm—" Her eyes went to the sling supporting Teaspoon's arm.

"Took a bullet—flesh wound. Lestways, it ain't my shootin' arm."

A mixture of worry and anger crimped Dulcie's forehead as she gazed past the three Indians flanking Teaspoon. "What about Toby and Sims?" She didn't bother to hide the anxiety in her voice and braced herself for the worst.

Teaspoon said, "Sorry to say, Sims went down in the stampede. Toby and I laid him to rest early this morning."

The Indian chief urged his pinto forward. He swept his arm toward the mountain. "One small child found this." The sinewy but powerfully built man held his hand toward Donovan. "My people no want trouble from the law. We come to ask your help."

Donovan accepted the tin star with a bullet hole through the center and turned it over in his hand. "United States Deputy Marshal," he read aloud, and cocked a dubious brow. "What about the body?"

Chief Three Feather's voice was shaded with worry. "We covered what was left with rocks to keep animals away." He pointed to his forehead and then to his breastplate. "Bullet hole here and here. You ride to Fort Apache and tell Ind'an agent, we good Apache. No kill lawman."

So this is what happened to Bert Nolan. Too bad. "I believe he was Bert Nolan. Marshal Cahill will want to know. When did you find the body?"

"One sunrise ago. The children were picking berries." The old chief spoke rapidly. "We hear spirit woman's screams, then hear much shooting. Night spirits say wait till morning."

"Yup, lucky the chief and his braves happened along. Six of his men are helping Toby round up the herd . . . lestways, what's left of 'em." Teaspoon conjured up a smile on his wrinkled face.

Pain caused Dulcie's stomach muscles to constrict, and her mouth went suddenly dry. She was so tired the revolver she held felt too heavy for her hand.

"Donovan . . ." A buzzing droned inside Dulcie's head.

Pressed against his chest, she felt the vibrations of Donovan's deep timbre voice. "Chief, how far to your village?"

"Woman sick?"

"Not exactly. She's with child."

"Know shortcut. Follow me."

Donovan removed the pistol that Dulcie still clutched and stuck it inside his waistband. "Hold tight, Dulcie."

The band rode swiftly, following the Apache chief across the rough terrain until he held up his hand signaling them to stop.

"What is it . . . why are we stopping?" Donovan spoke sharply.

"We wait for sun god to open mountain." Chief Three Feathers' face issued an exaggeratedly patient look at Donovan.

In spite of the heat, Dulcie gave a slight shiver that caused Donovan to glance at her worriedly and wonder if she had a fever. She seemed unaware of her surroundings as she gazed fixedly in the distance.

Donovan watched the shadow of the sun move across the face of the mountain until a jagged fissure was visible.

"Must hurry." Chief Three Fingers spurred his pinto. The animal reared and lunged forward into a gallop.

Donovan held tight to Dulcie. He gave the gray gelding its head, allowing the horse to stretch to its full stride.

Teaspoon and the braves closed the gap. Single file, the group rode into the Superstition Mountain's ancient passageway known only to the Apache and their ancestors.

Chapter Twenty-one

Inside the tepee, Donovan knelt beside Dulcie. "I've sent Toby and the chief's son to Fort Apache. It's only right Marshal Cahill knows what happened to his deputy. Toby's to ask the marshal to ride back here and to bring the Indian agent."

Dulcie grabbed at his sleeve. Her lower lip trembled.

Don't cry, he pleaded silently, *please don't cry.* He couldn't bear it when a female broke down and wept. "Red Fern Woman will take good care of you."

Dulcie blinked back the tears. "I'm not crying. The smoke, it bothers my eyes."

In the spill of moonlight seeping through the conical roof, she saw him smiling.

"You're leaving too?"

"Something isn't right, Dulcie. There's plenty of cattle herds crossing the Superstition Mountains. According to the chief, they all seem to mysteriously disappear before reaching Fort Apache. Chief Three Feathers and his people are starving. My gut instinct tells me that Humphrey is behind this."

"How will you prove it?"

Donovan shrugged a broad shoulder. "Don't know yet."

He reached around and grabbed his saddlebag. He removed a revolver that didn't have a firing pin. He used the tip of his knife to work a rolled piece of paper from the barrel and handed the document to Dulcie.

A puzzled frown wrinkled her smooth brow as she accepted the tightly rolled paper. "What is it?"

"A gambler doesn't always hold the winning hand, Dulcie. You'll have to trust my word that I didn't cheat your husband. Jack Slaughter signed over the deed to the Circle S of his own free will. The first day I rode into the yard and you trained your rifle sights on me, I knew I had no rights to the ranch."

"I don't understand. Why didn't you tell me?"

"Would you have believed me?"

She clamped down on her lip and shook her head.

"When you offered me the job of trail bossing your herd, I thought maybe I could make it right for leaving you a widow. I'd planned all along to give the deed to you once the cattle were sold. Then I'd move on."

Dulcie took his hand and held it to her heart. Even though he knew it was from gratitude and not affection, he treasured the sensation.

"Take care of yourself . . . and the little one when it gets here. Be it girl or boy." He might have had sandpaper in his throat, the way it sounded.

He rose and pushed the flap aside, and as he stepped through the opening, Dulcie said, very softly, "Thank you, Donovan."

She smiled and closed her eyes, none too soon. The tenderness he felt toward her was overwhelming and bound to show on his face, and he didn't want her to see it.

Sitting cross-legged around the council fire, Donovan passed the peace pipe to Teaspoon. Donovan flicked his eyes toward the shaman. "We've all heard the screams and seen the strange bouncing lights in the mountains. Did you ever send men to investigate?"

The wizened old man's voice took on a singsong cadence. "We call on Nagi Tanka, the Great Spirit, to protect our young warriors. Only Black Elk return. Before he die, he say *kagi*, demon, kill young men." The old man passed his hand over the fire and blue flames shot upward.

Donovan heaved to his feet. He paced with a catlike restlessness. "Like the Comanche, the Apache are fierce, not filled with *kokipa*."

Chief Three Feathers spoke. "In Comanche your name means 'strong warrior.' We have few young men. I am old, and yes, my people fear the screaming woman. She is angry because Apache no keep white eyes from sacred mountains."

The shaman rose to place his hand on Donovan's shoulder. "Strong Warrior, I have called upon the Great Spirit Nagi Tanka to send us a leader. In you, he has answered my prayer."

Teaspoon chuckled. "Looks like you done got yourself in a fine pickle, Donovan. What you gonna do about it?"

Donovan's mouth twisted into a wry grin. He sat and crossed his legs, then leaned forward to lay out his plan.

"Let me get the straight of this, Donovan. What you're saying is there ain't no screamin' woman, and there ain't no evil spirits? That means we're all a little tetched in the head, 'cause we none of us saw them dancing lights neither?" Teaspoon gestured with his hands. "Danged if'n I ain't plumb confused."

There were times when Donovan's Irish and Comanche blood and the beliefs of his father and mother warred within him. He'd long ago figured out that the true evil in the world came from men like Clive Humphrey. He cast a challenge at each Apache seated around the fire. To discount the shaman's words and to make him appear foolish was not the way to enlist the help of Chief Three Feathers.

Donovan reminded himself that except for Humphrey, he'd avenged the deaths of his father and brother. And he intended to bring Humphrey to his knees, but not with a bullet. Just like he'd witnessed his family's hanging, he'd watch Humphrey swing at the end of a rope.

"Chief, if Toby and your son make good time, they should return in a fortnight with Marshal Cahill. It'd go in your favor if we solve the mystery of Deputy Nolan's death before the marshal gets here."

Chief Three Feathers' brows knitted into a bronzed frown. "You make plenty sense, Donovan. At dawn, I show you where lawman's body found. Tonight we will eat and then sleep so we go into battle strong."

Suddenly drained of his energy, Donovan admitted to himself a cooked meal was welcome and extra hours of rest were probably even better. With the hard riding and the abrasions on his chest, he could use a step backward and a fresh start to brace for what lay ahead.

"Shaman cast the spirit bones. Ask Nagi Tanka to show us where the screaming woman sleeps. Ask the Great Spirit to make us invisible so the *kagi* demons cannot attack us. And when we ride out of camp, sing our victory song."

Grunting his acknowledgment to Donovan's request, the shaman chanted as he drew a powder from his medicine pouch and blew it into the fire. The tepee filled with white smoke.

Donovan studied the back trail over his shoulder as they rode. He noticed the hard set to the chief's mouth as they wound away from the camp to steeper land. There had been no conversation since leaving in the still darkness.

As dawn pinked the gray clouds, Donovan's head turned partly to one side. He stood in the stirrups. The chief followed the direction of his gaze and then looked at him, as if waiting for Donovan to say something.

"I saw some birds light off from up in the trees a ways back. That might mean something. We'll check it after you've shown me where you found the deputy's body."

They reined in and dismounted in a patch of briars and wild strawberries. Narrowing his eyes, Donovan studied the area with care, a searching study, missing no bush, no rock. He used the toe of his boot to lift a bush. Two frightened rabbits skittered between his legs.

"You figured out what you're looking for, Trail Boss?" Teaspoon fingered the reins in his gnarled hand.

Narrowing his eyes against the morning light, Donovan said, "Nolan wasn't killed here."

"Don't say. How'd you know?"

"Even after these many months, there should be some sign. Maybe a blemish on a rock, new growth on broken twigs." Donovan shrugged. He set his toe in the stirrup and swung into the saddle. At a dip in the trail they reined to the left and began to climb.

"There." Chief Three Feathers pointed. "Nagi Tanka sends a sign. We ride where the eagle soars."

Donovan cast a cautious glance at the old wrangler riding alongside. "This high up, voices will carry."

"Don't have to tell me twice, Trail Boss. I'll keep my pie-hole shut."

Donovan led the way into a hollow. To the left the land sloped down to meet the base of another set of hills, and to the other side, higher ground spotted with trees and laced with trails led to the hollow. The troop rode north until they curled back to the east on the far side of the ridge up ahead.

Teaspoon pushed his pony alongside Donovan. He motioned for him to lean in close. In the barest of whispers he said, "Rockin' H." He lifted both hands, closed and shut his fist three times, and then pointed upward at the eagle that rose and dipped in a graceful ballet.

A muscle ticked beneath Donovan's right eye as he nodded his understanding. As the eagle flies, Humphrey's ranch lay thirty miles to the east.

The mountains were filled with shortcuts. Humphrey would know this. He would also know of hidden canyons, places to hide large herds of stolen cattle. And he'd play on the Apaches' superstitions to keep them out of the area. *Smart,* Donovan thought. *Humphrey is nobody's fool.*

Within a few minutes, the tortuous trail took them to rocky ground broken by bevels and steep ledges. They still climbed upward. Across the shelf to the north was an incline half covered with trees, but the ground itself was fairly level all the way up. The area was littered with mounds. The smell of death lingered.

Chief Three Feathers hauled up on the reins of his pinto. He used sign language to say they would go no further. This was a place of evil.

From his time with the Comanche, Donovan knew all tribes buried their insane or mentally ill or those born with physical deformities in remote places. They were buried at night without ceremony so their spirits could not harm the living.

Chief Three Feathers signed, "No go." And then he followed with "*Kagi,*" the word for "demons."

Donovan extended his arm. He signed the word *cave.* And then he signaled for Teaspoon to follow. He and the old wrangler turned across the shelf and made for the slope.

The Apache followed.

Donovan rounded a shoulder with the harsh realization of how unsure he was—unsure as to how many gunmen there might be. A few yards further on, he stopped and sniffed the air. A hint of cigarette smoke wafted on the breeze.

He squinted across the span until his eyes discerned two figures seated in the shadows at the mouth of a fissure. He swung out of the saddle. Teaspoon and the warriors followed his example, clasping their rifles, keeping an eye on the men below.

Donovan kept his voice low as he gestured down the slope. "That looks like Frank Lowe down there."

Teaspoon squinted pensively. "Yep, and it's a sure bet

t'others are with him." He tapped his injured arm with the barrel of his shotgun. "Pete Garvey's mine. I owe him one."

Two more men stepped from the shadows. Donovan strained to hear their words, but the span was too far.

About half a distance away, Donovan and Teaspoon spotted three riders galloping across a valley. Teaspoon huffed a whisper, "I recognize that roan. It's one of ours."

Donovan back-stepped into the shadows of the trees. "Chief, you know if there's a back door to that cave?"

The man grunted. "Follow me." He hefted himself up on the pinto's back and turned the horse toward a patch of wooded hills that bordered the outlaws' hiding place.

The high sun poured a sharp, even light on the grassy flatland. Chief Three Feathers held up his hand to halt the riders as they rounded a hill shorn abruptly on one side. He signaled that there was a space between the two formations. He pointed upward. "Steep climb."

Lean, wind-whipped, and savage, Donovan nodded his understanding. "We'll leave the horses here. Less chance of being heard." He motioned for the men to dismount. Birds darted through trees like arrows, and the deep green belt of foliage provided a good cover for the horses.

"Say, Trail Boss, you hear what I hear?" Teaspoon's question was quick and muted.

The bawling of several hundred beeves filtered through an opening leading to a hidden canyon.

"Wonder how many of those steers are wearing the Circle S brand?" Donovan glanced up at the eagle circling in the distance, arching around and around where peaks shot up against the sky. "Unless I miss my guess, Humphrey's behind this operation."

Teaspoon slapped his thigh. "If'n he is, I'll tear him from limb to limb for what he's put Miz Dulcie through."

"Right after I finish with him." Donovan uncorked his canteen and drew on it. He offered it to the chief.

"Good hiding place. Apache not come this far. Have to cross demon burial grounds to get here."

Donovan knew better than to make light of Chief Three Feathers' superstitions. "The shaman has made strong medicine."

"Yes. Him make us invisible."

There was time for Donovan and his companions to catch their wind and refresh themselves with quick bites of jerky. He opened his saddlebag and filled his pocket with spare .45 cartridges, then slipped a knife into the lining of his boot. Handing him the canteen, he clapped Teaspoon on the shoulder. "Stay with horses or climb. Your choice, ol'-timer."

With an indignant *pshaw,* Teaspoon jammed buckshot shells into his pocket. "Ain't gonna baby-sit broomtails and miss all the fun, that's for dang sure."

An hour later the winding trail took them to the backside of the cave. Donovan checked on the old wrangler. Teaspoon was puffing and grimacing but holding his own.

Panting himself, Donovan spent time catching his breath when Chief Three Feathers signaled for the party to halt.

They drew up at the base of a hill and stared. The high sun poured a sharp light on the cave's back entrance, exposing an opening large enough for a man to walk through, yet narrow enough to blend with its surroundings. A small corral held two saddled horses. No one stood guard. Tracks leading in and out indicated a regular flow of movement from the rear entrance.

The sound of laughter and men's voices echoed through the cleft. Donovan strategically positioned the warriors. Teaspoon and Chief Three Feathers followed him through the slit. From their vantage point the front opening was visible. With backs turned away from Donovan and his party, Frank Lowe sat at a makeshift table. He and a thin man with lanky yellow hair shared a game of cards.

Donovan signaled for quiet. He pointed at two canvas-covered crates. He lifted the corner of a tarp to examine the contents and was met with a fierce and unexpected snarl.

Donovan and his companions hugged the wall when Lowe shifted to look over his shoulder. The gunman said, "How long's it been since you fed the cats?"

"Long enough. 'Sides, the hungrier they are, the louder they yowl when they try gettin' at that poor lil fox and her kit."

The yellow-haired man whipped a knife from the sheath at his waist and played it back and forth in front of Lowe's face, all the time chuckling. "Maybe I'll cut you up and feed you to 'em."

Lowe stood. "Humphrey sure called it right when he sent you up here. You're loco."

Vesper's hand snaked out. He tipped the knife blade under Lowe's chin. "You sayin' I'm crazy?"

Lowe slapped the knife hand away. His voice was balanced between challenge and casualness. "As a rabid dog. Now go feed them cats."

Chapter Twenty-two

Donovan and his crew stepped back and made themselves small against the dark cool walls. As the straggly haired man shuffled tentatively toward him, Donovan braced himself with the thought that his luck had been fairly good so far. He reached down and withdrew the knife from his boot. He tensed his legs, balancing all his weight on the balls of his feet.

The man called Vesper lifted the lid on a barrel. Donovan's stomach roiled against the odor of putrid meat.

Vesper gagged audibly. He grabbed a bottle from a ledge above the barrel and turned it to his lips. After a long draught, he coughed and drew the back of his hand across his mouth. "Damn, stinkin' . . ." He followed with a string of curse words. He threw the bottle against the wall. Glass shattered. "We're outta rotgut, Lowe. Next time you ride to the ranch, bring a case. Only thing keeps me sane."

A sardonic chuckle echoed through the cave. "You wouldn't know sane if it jumped up and bit you in the—"

Vesper emitted a growl. "Shut your hole, Lowe."

Grabbing a long pole, Vesper reached down and flipped the canvas back with a hard thrust, revealing two large cages on either side of a smaller cage.

In echo after echo, shrill screams reverberated against the walls of the cave, stiffening the hairs on the back of Donovan's neck. Muscles along his back bunched.

"Jehawzafat almighty." Teaspoon's voice flushed with fear.

Chief Three Feathers called out to the Great Spirit Nagi Tanka to save them from the screaming woman.

The element of surprise lost, Donovan sprang forward in a single motion, grabbed the yellow-haired man's face, and spun him around. With the other hand he gripped a shoulder and drove the man hard toward the wall, jerking up just before contact. Vesper's head thudded in a fast-glancing collision. The body slumped and Donovan let the deadweight drop to the ground.

Several voices came from inside the cave. Donovan's eyes raked toward the entrance and off to the side as shadows scurried forward.

Bullets sang past both sides as Donovan dashed for the rear entrance. He squeezed off two shots. Chips of granite flew through the air to sting his face.

"Teaspoon . . . Chief . . . get outta here!"

Coming at them was an intermittent flash from a Winchester muzzle. Blasts returned from a shotgun's twin barrels.

"You hit, Teaspoon?" When Donovan spoke it was a coiled whisper.

"Nope. You?"

"Not yet."

Outside, gunfire spat fitfully, the roar of the shots slapping back and forth from both Apache and outlaws. Donovan called out, "Lowe?"

"Yeah?"

"Give it up and I'll see you get a fair shake with the law."

The outlaw answered with a volley of gunfire. Donovan sprang to the opposite corner. Shots mingled with the piercing screams of the panicked pumas and foxes caught in the cross fire.

Bullets gouged the cave walls and whined overhead. Crouching low, Donovan scuttled to the back corner. The gun smoke stung his eyes and seared his lungs. Teaspoon and the chief wheeled and raced through the cleft that opened to the outside.

Donovan zigzagged close on their heels. He squeezed off the last load in his Colt and jumped behind a boulder to eject the spent shells and reload. He stiffened. Something hit him in the small of his back.

He turned, "Teaspoon, did you—?"

Then it came again, a tiny pebble, and this time it bounced off his shoulder from above.

Donovan, pulse racing, looked up while thumbing in his second cartridge to see Pete Garvey standing on an outcrop and leering down at him. Another pebble fell.

"He's mine." Teaspoon's voice was low but far-carrying.

The shotgun blast sent an echoing crescendo across the mountainside. The outlaw yowled and staggered sideways, gripping his leg above the knee.

Teaspoon yelled out, "Dagnabit . . . missed!"

Slugs whizzed past in a thick barrage. Donovan snapped off two shots, the impact spinning Garvey around before he toppled off the cave's roof to the basin below.

"Hold yer fire!" a voice called out from behind a rock.

Donovan hissed, "Throw out your weapons . . . hands high."

Pike and then Chapman tossed their pistols into view. Pike gripped Chapman under the left armpit. Donovan saw the dark, spreading patch on the man's right shoulder.

Gunfire fell silent. The damage had been done. The mountain had become horribly quiet. There was a look of profound disarray to the scene where bodies lay tangled and sprawled on the hard ground.

Donovan's stomach knotted. The lines around the mouth and eyes of the Apache chief seemed deeply scored.

"Teaspoon, get a rope on those two."

"What about my arm?" Chapman whined.

"What about it?" Donovan's face was drawn tight and stony.

"There's more'n just us. Humphrey'll hear the shots and

bring reinforcements." Chapman turned to the man propping him up. "Tell 'em, Pike."

"Shut up, Chapman." Pike grimaced as the old wrangler jerked his arms behind his back, binding his wrist and tightening the knot. Pike slid to the ground.

Teaspoon said to Chapman, "Gimme your bandanna. Make your mama proud and stop your whimperin'." The outlaw used his good hand to unknot the square of cloth from around his neck.

A burst of bullets ricocheted off a boulder on the high ground, striking a rock behind Donovan. He caught a glimpse of Mayo moving across a stone lip. Donovan hammered back the trigger of his Colt. Instead of bucking in his hand, it answered with a click. His eyes narrowed as he opened the Colt's chamber to reload while he scanned the outcrop above him.

Donovan answered Chief Three Feathers' signal with a nod. The Apache brought his Winchester up and levered from the hip. Mayo loomed on the ledge, teetering in a delicate balance and then dropping heavily. The body hit the ground like a sack of potatoes, rolled off, and spun down the hill to sprawl to a stop at Donovan's boots.

In a soft voice, Pike said, "It's over. Mayo was the last."

It was midnight and their horses were winded when Donovan and his exhausted companions hit the brushy clearing. He hunched his tired shoulders against the night's chill. A growing irritation coursed through him as he made a conscious effort to sort out what had happened over the past four days. His body yearned for rest.

As soon as he settled his final score with Humphrey and finished his obligation to Dulcie, he would be gone, leaving behind the vengeance that had eaten away at him like a disease.

With this promise to himself, the exhilaration he had once

felt at tracking the men who'd murdered his family and then eliminating them was now fading fast.

Dulcie was frightened, though she tried not to admit it to herself. All morning she had felt a change at work within her body. Her time was at hand.

Red Fern Woman tossed a log on the fire. Sparks spiraled upward to the small ventilation hole in the tepee. A merry glow cast shadows on the walls with flickering shades of orange.

"The little one grows restless."

Needing to drive the worry from her mind, Dulcie thought talking might help. "Where did you learn to speak English?"

Red Fern Woman offered a patient smile. "From Yellow Horse, my son. He learned at the agency school. It is good thing, yes?"

Dulcie shifted her swollen form to a more comfortable position. A moment to catch her breath, a moment more to feel the life force within her stir before another spasm caused her to bite down on her knuckles to keep from crying out. "Yes, it is a good thing." She tried to drive the worry from her mind. She wished Donovan and Teaspoon would return. She shivered and sighed. She uttered a small gasp and waited for the pain to subside.

"You must breathe in deep and let it out slow. It will lessen the pain."

"How many children do you have, Red Fern Woman?"

The woman held up her hand with five splayed fingers. "All gone now. Only Yellow Horse remains to carry on his father's legacy."

Dulcie saw the sadness in the older woman's ebony eyes and wanted to inquire about the other children. What had happened to them? Instead she doubled forward in agony. She did as Red Fern Woman instructed and breathed in, exhaled slowly, and found by doing so the pain did lessen.

Panic clutched her heart in an iron grip. She whimpered and bit her knuckles. Not now, she prayed, not here. *Donovan, Teaspoon, where are you?* What woman wasn't afraid when her time came? A voice seemed to whisper, *I am not a child to be afraid.* And yet, children were born every day and under much more primitive conditions.

But now? Alone? No, she wasn't alone. Red Fern Woman was with her. The panic lessened although the fear remained. And sadness plagued her. Why hadn't she stayed in New York? Still, she didn't regret the decision to leave. She wished Red Fern Woman would mix a potion to lessen the pain.

Dulcie took the tightly rolled paper from her reticule and opened it. The deed to the Circle S. A bundle of emotions overwhelmed her. Anger at Donovan, anger at Jack Slaughter, and anger at herself and the predicament she was in. She slipped the document back inside its hiding place.

She almost lost consciousness, so severe was the next cramp.

"Help me, Red Fern Woman," she gasped. "I don't think I can bear much more."

The Apache woman lifted a bowl to Dulcie's lips. "Drink."

Dulcie grimaced at the acrid taste. "What is it?"

"It is medicinal tea to ensure an easy delivery." She tipped the bowl again. "Do not fear, Dul-cee."

Again the pain eased.

She watched Red Fern Woman take a small flint knife from an oiled skin and hold the blade over the smoldering embers.

"What is the knife for?"

"With this I will cut the cord of life." She unfolded a swath of brushed buckskin. "And this is to keep the infant from getting a chill." She placed beside the cloth a pouch containing a fine powder derived from the prairie puffball to dust the babe before bundling it in the soft wrappings. Red Fern Woman handed Dulcie a thick length of twisted rawhide. "Place this between your teeth."

With trembling fingers Dulcie obeyed and bit down in time to keep from screaming as the next series of contractions struck. She closed her eyes and listened to her own rasping breath. How long she remained like this she could not tell. Was it the pain? She heard something. Was she going mad?

She listened, concentrated . . . yes . . . a chant . . . only in her mind . . . it must be in her mind . . . only because she was frightened . . . but heard still . . . the voices of women seemed to fill the room. She trembled and kept her eyes tightly closed.

Red Fern Woman whispered, "It is the Birthing Song. It tells of dying ways. It tells of how the strength of a people is in the children. It tells of courage. And salvation in the land. It tells of the love of man and woman and the child who would mirror such love."

Dulcie listened. But she hadn't loved Jack Slaughter. After the first flush of enthusiasm had passed, he had proved something other than what she had read in his letters. And when he'd ridden away to buy supplies, she had no idea whether she'd ever see him again. She'd made him her means of escape from a life of drudgery only to end up here, alone and miles from civilization.

Red Fern Woman touched the gold band on Dulcie's finger. "Your man will return soon. He is strong like *nahkohe,* the bear."

Dulcie's pain-glazed eyes stared into a pair of ebony marbles. "My husband is dead."

"The one called Donovan—he is not your man?"

Dulcie didn't want to talk. She clamped down on the rawhide against another spasm. "No. He's the reason my husband is dead."

Red Fern Woman responded with a low grunt as she removed the leather strip from Dulcie's teeth. She tilted the bowl. "Drink."

Dulcie shook her head. "It's bitter."

"Drink." Red Fern Woman's voice remained soft but commanding.

Unable to control the grimace, Dulcie reluctantly obeyed.

"Close your eyes and listen to the Birthing Song. It will soothe you."

Red Fern Woman clapped her hands together and rubbed the heat across Dulcie's distended abdomen. "The little one is ready to greet the world."

"How much longer?"

Placing a cool cloth across Dulcie's forehead, Red Fern Woman smiled. "Soon."

"I'm afraid."

"Rest your fears. The Great Spirit is with you."

Dulcie endured until the chant faded, becoming one with the groaning chorus of the wind.

Perspiration beaded her forehead. She accepted the strange remedies of Red Fern Woman without further resistance.

She drifted between pain and dreams. She was back in New York. A woodchopper came in with his ax and crossed the room. The ax was raised but came down with incredible, excruciating slowness. As it reached halfway, the ax seemed to waver in the air and Dulcie was suddenly beneath it, staring at the oncoming blade.

Her screams filled the tepee as pain ripped through her body.

Chapter Twenty-three

At the top of a crest Donovan's crew and their prisoners halted the horses and looked down into the wooded valley on the other side of a creek. Smoke from a campfire showed at the treetops in the middle of the distance.

Chief Three Feathers nudged his pinto alongside Donovan's gray. He pointed toward the remuda. "My son's pony."

Donovan's eyes followed and rested on the black-and-white Tobiano. A yellow dun and two bay horses stood out among the ragged calico Indian ponies. "I recognize Toby's horse. Not the two bays."

Cold fingers clawed at Donovan's insides. His eyes strayed to the tepee where he'd left Dulcie. "We've been gone four days. Too soon for Toby and Yellow Horse to make it to the fort and back. Maybe they ran into trouble."

Chief Three Feathers grunted. "Me find out."

"Hope you got some tarantula juice stashed in one of them tepees, Chief. This wound in my shoulder is screamin'," Chapman lamented dramatically.

Donovan glanced over in time to see Teaspoon cuff Chapman on the back of the head. The old wrangler scowled at the outlaw. "Dagnabit, hesh up your piehole."

The chief motioned with his rifle to a man and barked an order in Apache. "I tell Spotted Owl to scout village. We wait."

They watched the scout push down the other side of the

slope to work slowly toward the base of the wood where a thin trail wound inward.

The stretch of ground between the creek and the village was mottled with angular shadows cast by the last vestiges of moonlight. Only the sound of a horse stamping its hoof or the swish of a tail to ward off an insect broke the silence.

A brown cur ambled across the encampment, stopped, sniffed the air, then ambled out of sight. Donovan never took his eyes off the Apache scout.

"What's going to happen to us, Trail Boss?" Pike asked impatiently.

Donovan studied his youngish face. Pike looked like a man who was going to be sick. Like a schoolkid caught cheating. "Murder . . . cattle rustling . . . reckon a judge and jury will figure it all out."

"I know plenty about Humphrey. If I testify, you think things'll go easy for me?"

"How old are you, Pike?"

The outlaw shrugged his shoulders. "Ain't exactly for sure, twenty-seven, maybe."

Twenty-seven. Donovan suddenly felt older than his own thirty-two years.

"Old enough, I reckon."

"Old enough for what, Donovan?"

"To choose the company you run with . . . old enough to hang for making bad choices."

Pike's sigh was deep and heavy. His chin sagged to his chest.

Chapman said, "Buck up, kid. I got me a bet."

"Yeah, what's that?"

"Got me a bet that if I get my hand on a gun, I can kill Donovan, the old man, and the chief before any of 'em can clear leather."

"Shut up, Chapman." Pike glared at the wounded man.

"You talk a good fight," Donovan said.

"Wanna call my hand? One thing I promise, if I don't kill you dead with my first shot, I'll leave you lay for the buzzards to pick clean."

Donovan sat the gray gelding in silence. His unreadable blue eyes studied the outlaw. "Nothing would give me more pleasure than to call you out, Chapman." He harrumphed. "You're not worth it."

Yellow teeth showed in Chapman's brindle-stubbled face. He licked his lips then leaned sideways, reaching toward his boot. "Danged if I ain't got the foot rot somethin' fierce. Got me an itch 'tween my toes that just won't quit."

Without warning, he spurred his horse. The startled gelding rammed into Donovan's gray. Chapman lunged, body-slamming Donovan from the saddle.

"Hold it, sapsucker. Drop that toadsticker. At this range buckshot'll make a mess of you." Teaspoon sighted down the shotgun's twin barrels.

Donovan's deep voice snapped, "He wants a fight, Teaspoon, he's got it."

Chapman held his bound hands forward.

"Drop the knife first." Teaspoon shifted the shotgun's barrel toward the weapon Chapman gripped.

Chapman licked his lips again as he tossed the blade into the ground.

Donovan unsheathed the long Bowie at his belt. "Cut his hands loose, Chief."

Remaining mounted, Chief Three Feathers sliced through the ropes as Chapman held up his hands.

After flexing his fingers and shaking out his wrists as if to pump circulation back into his hands, Chapman grabbed his knife. He played it back and forth.

Grinning thinly, he said, "Piece by piece, Donovan, I'm gonna peel your hide."

The blade glinted in the morning light. Chapman stepped forward, thrusting out until the knife's point touched Donovan's belly. "You know what I figure I might do? I figure I might gut you. I know how to do it."

Donovan didn't flinch when the tip of Chapman's knife pierced his shirt and bit into his flesh. He feinted left, shifting the Bowie from his left hand to the right hand, slashing in one swift movement. The front of Chapman's shirt dissolved in red as the knife carved deep.

"Why . . . ," Chapman began, his grin sliding to a painful scowl. "Why, I'll—" His boot lashed forward, striking Donovan on the wrist, the blow sending the Bowie flying from Donovan's grip.

Chapman waded in for the kill. Donovan used all his strength to imprison the hand that held the formidable weapon. In a dance of death, the men locked together like two bulls.

Donovan used a Comanche wrestling move to trip Chapman. The stocky man landed with a thud. Donovan dove for the Bowie, grasped it, and then landed on his feet with the agility of a cat.

Chapman's mouth twisted.

Pike yelled, "Donovan, look out!"

Chapman raked a fistful of dirt and tossed it into Donovan's eyes. Chapman's voice was low and hard. "Yer next, Pike."

Donovan clawed to clear his vision. His eyes watered, turning the dust to mud. Squinting, he caught a flicker of a movement. Instinctively his hands reached out to parry the attack.

Panting from exhaustion, the stench of sweat oozed from their bodies as they grappled under the August rays. Towering a foot taller than the outlaw, Donovan called on all his strength to shove the blade away from his throat. Blood dribbled down his cheek. Inch by excruciating inch, he forced the knife lower.

Chapman growled and grunted in an effort to hold on to his leverage. He rasped, "I'll see you in hell, Donovan."

At that instant a strange thing happened: a puma's scream startled both horses and riders.

Chief Three Feather's pinto reared. A hoof struck Chapman on the shoulder, knocking the outlaw against Donovan. Chapman's face dissolved in unbelievable astonishment as he simply fell forward, the knife embedding deep into his chest as he landed heavily atop Donovan.

In a quick motion, Donovan shoved the lifeless body aside. He drank in large gulps of air, then brushed a sleeve across his face to clear his eyes.

Teaspoon hustled out of the saddle and offered his canteen to Donovan. "Hoowee. If that ain't the dangest thing I ever did see."

"Screaming Woman. She sought her revenge."

Donovan drew deep from the canteen. He untied the bandanna from around his neck and moistened it to wipe the blood from his cheekbone. "No, Chief. More than likely it's the puma we let loose a few days ago. I imagine after months of being caged and kept half-starved, she's looking for a fresh kill."

Chief Three Feathers cast a sidelong glance at Donovan. "Think as you wish, Comanche brother."

Donovan motioned to Pike. "Grab up Chapman's horse and help me heft this piece of trash across the saddle."

"We ain't burying him?"

Donovan sucked in another deep breath to ease his exhaustion. The air was sultry and sweat trickled down his face. There was no breeze.

He pointed toward the village where activity gathered. "Uh-uh, evidence. Unless I miss my guess, that's Spotted Owl signaling for us to come in, and standing next to him is Marshal Cahill and the sheriff from Blountstown."

While securing Chapman's body to the saddle, Donovan said, "How many men you kill for Humphrey?"

The question seemed to startle Pike. His Adam's apple

worked up and down as if trying to conjure up enough spittle to answer the question. "None . . . not the first man. Sure I rustled cattle and I took my turn up at the cave with Vesper and Smitty, but I never put a bullet in nobody . . . leastways that I know of."

"What about stampedes, Pike? How many innocent men died in stampedes that you helped start?"

Pike leaned his head against the gelding's shoulder. "I ain't going to make any excuses for what I done. It wasn't right. I know it. Reckon I got a lot to own up to."

Donovan was slow to answer, clearly not used to this sort of confession. "I owe you for the warning. Tell the marshal what you know—and I mean everything—about Humphrey, and I'll see if I can make things go light for you."

Pike darted a glance at the man across from him.

Donovan accepted the reins from Teaspoon and, setting his toe in the stirrup, swung up on the gray. He met Pike's eyes. "I'm not tying your hands, Pike, but try to run and I'll put a bullet in you."

There was a feeling that he should be hurrying to do something, but when he thought about it he didn't know what his plans were. He supposed the thing to do was settle with the marshal and sheriff, make plans to capture Humphrey, and then check on Dulcie.

Chapter Twenty-four

Y ou look like a man who's been rode hard and put up wet."

"Howdy, Marshal Cahill." Donovan stepped down from the saddle. He thumbed toward Pike. "Man draped across the sorrel is Chapman."

"You kill him?"

"In a manner of speaking." Donovan briefly outlined the knife fight.

Marshal Cahill walked around and grabbed a hank of the dead man's hair and lifted upward. "Yep, recognize him. Got a poster with a reward of a thousand dollars, dead or alive. You can claim it anytime. Come by my office and sign a few papers first."

"We buried four more up on the mountain."

"Names?" The marshal pulled a pad and a pencil stub from his vest pocket. He licked the end of the pencil.

"Don't know their given names . . . Vesper, Smitty, Lowe, and Mayo. All Humphrey's men."

Flies hummed around the body that had already begun to bloat from the heat. Toby stepped forward. "Sure good to see you, Donovan. Yellow Horse and I will take care of the burying."

He thanked the boy and watched as Toby took the reins from Pike and led the horse away.

Chief Three Feathers spoke to his son. "Tell Red Fern Woman to bring food, much food to the council lodge."

As they followed the chief, Donovan said, "Marshal, I

surely hope that either you or the sheriff brought along coffee."

Cahill grinned. "Never travel without it or a pot to brew it in."

After they were all seated around the council fire, the chief said, "We eat, we talk, then we go to sweat lodge to purge evil spirits from our bodies, and then we sleep."

Dulcie first, then sleep. "We'll make plans to take Humphrey down." Donovan shifted his gaze to each lawman. "I want him alive. After I finish with Humphrey, you can fight over who hangs him."

Donovan drew a long, controlled breath. "I'm curious to know how you and Sheriff Horn ended up here before Toby and Yellow Horse had a chance to get to the fort."

While Cahill measured out coffee grounds into his pot, Sheriff Horn said, "Sam here rode into Blountstown looking for his deputy. He also told me about the trouble you'd run into with Humphrey's men. I decided to ride along with him, thinking we'd catch up with you on the trail. Instead we ran into Toby and the chief's son. They explained about the stampede and how you'd brought Mrs. Slaughter to the village, so we followed the boys here. Got in last night. I wanted to square things about you with Mrs. Slaughter." Horn grinned. "She was a might busy."

"Guess Toby told you about the village children finding Nolan's body?" Donovan wondered what would keep a white woman busy in an Apache camp. He didn't ask.

Marshal Cahill said, "Hated to hear about Bert. He had a wife and boy. Tough to lose a good man." He used his knife to stir the coffee grounds. "All the more reason to bring Humphrey in alive. It'd pleasure me to watch him hang."

He cast a look toward Pike. "Donovan says you're willing to testify against Humphrey."

"Yes, sir."

"You'd best tell it now, in case things go wrong once we're at Humphrey's ranch."

Donovan reached forward and poured a round of coffee. Everyone in the circle listened to Pike as Marshal Cahill made notes in his pad.

While Pike talked, Donovan got a glimpse of the gentler side of the younger man. It seemed apparent he'd had a good upbringing. Like himself, circumstances played a significant role in the path he'd chosen.

It wasn't until Marshal Cahill spoke his name a second time that Donovan realized he'd drifted away from the conversation.

"Donovan, you seem to have a personal score to settle with Humphrey. What's your beef with him?"

Fifteen years was a long time to live a nightmare. Ordering his thoughts, Donovan tamped down his emotions; even so, his voice quavered with hatred. "Small ranchers and farmers who wouldn't sell out to the railroad were paid visits by night riders. At first it was to put the fear of wrath into them. When that didn't work, houses and barns were torched, and then the hangings started. Jack Slaughter and Clive Humphrey were the leaders. Humphrey's money was made on the blood of people like my father and brother."

Donovan lifted the bowl. He grimaced at the bitter coffee gone cold. "The railroad wanted to pay us two dollars an acre. When the ranchers refused, the railroad claimed imminent domain.

"Our ranch wasn't even part of the property in the railroad's right of way. Lot of ranches weren't. Didn't much matter though.

"After pumping three slugs into me, Jack Slaughter put the lash to the horses, but it was Humphrey who gave the command. My father and brother were hanged for no reason other than greed and bloodlust."

Engulfed in anger, a soul-shuddering sigh wracked through Donovan. "Back then his name was Humfried . . . and he was the railroad's main enforcer."

"Where're you from, Donovan?"

"Utah."

Marshal Cahill pursed his lips as he stuffed the notepad and pencil into his vest pocket. "You're a long way from home, son."

"Even so, I'd travel from hell and back to get Humphrey."

"Hmm. Tom tells me you're Ace Donovan, the gambler."

Donovan shifted his eyes toward the sheriff. "That's right."

"You've put a few poker players in the ground."

"Five to be exact."

"Wouldn't be men who worked for the railroad and took their orders from Humphrey, would they?"

"You'd be right on both counts, Marshal. They were fair fights."

"I checked out each one."

Suspicion flew through Donovan's mind. He locked stares with the marshal.

Cahill nodded his understanding. "Can't say I wouldn't have done the same if I were wearing your boots."

The conversation ceased momentarily while women brought in bowls of wild potatoes, steamed mescal plant, and dried beef.

When the marshal spoke, his voice was calm and thoughtful. "Toby said Humphrey paid your cow camp a visit. He didn't recognize you?"

"I was seventeen years old the day he left me lying in the dirt. Time changes the way a man looks, Marshal."

Cahill chewed thoughtfully. "So it does."

After the women returned to remove the bowls, Chief Three Feathers said, "We go to sweat lodge now."

Outside, Donovan spied the smoke from the dome-shaped

wickiup. He hoped the temperature inside would help leech the anger from his heart. Whatever tomorrow brought, he'd meet it as he always had—head-on.

Donovan hesitated before stepping through the flap. A wrinkled, bronze face smiled up at him. Red Fern Woman placed a finger to her lips, then left the dwelling. A squalling protest issued from beneath a blanket.

Donovan spun around in time for Dulcie to poke her delicate features over the edge of the blanket. Something stirred beside her in the bedding and a tiny fist poked upward in defiance.

"Dulcie," Donovan gasped, kneeling beside the pallet. He rocked forward on his knees.

She smiled weakly. "I have a daughter."

He reached out to touch the bunched and wrinkled features, to stroke the honey-colored fuzz. The infant's tiny hand closed around Donovan's finger. Her cries subsided. She seemed content to snuggle in the loving hollow of her mother's arms.

"Her name is Maggie." A single tear gleamed in the corner of Dulcie's eye. She wiped it away with the back of her hand.

Donovan cleared his throat, uncertain of what to say. "She's not very big."

Dulcie lifted her eyes to his. She reached out to take his hand. "I'm in your debt."

"You should rest. I'll take my leave."

"Don't go. Sheriff Horn explained about the poker game, and . . . the shooting."

Donovan thought he saw her jaw tremble as she spoke. Lost for words, he merely nodded. His heart was both happy and heavy.

"Red Fern Woman said you brought in two men. One of them was dead."

Donovan eased from his knees to sit cross-legged. "Brought Chapman tied across a saddle. Pike was the other."

"Too bad Pike got mixed up with a gang of outlaws."

"Good or bad, a man makes his choices, Dulcie. In the end, he has to live with himself and the consequences."

"You're all flesh and blood, Donovan. Yet you're also a man of mystery. In all the weeks we've been on the trail, I know little about you. What about your choices? And . . . what happened on the mountain?"

He had no idea how to confront her. He hoped she'd appreciate honesty as he related the details of his life, his connection to Humphrey, and the shoot-out on top of the mountain. He caught himself staring at Dulcie.

She'd remained quiet while he explained, asking no questions, taking everything in. Donovan made a mental note that she seemed genuinely empathic and surprised.

"You mean those awful piercing cries that all of us thought was a woman being tortured were actually two pumas? I don't understand how those men got them to scream." Dulcie looked thoroughly perplexed.

Donovan smiled at the incredulous look on her face. "Easy enough. The cats were kept in a state of semistarvation. Sandwiched in between the two pumas' cages was a smaller pen with a fox and her kit. When it was time for the screaming woman to appear, Vesper or one of the other men at the cave would remove the canvas from the cages and the hungry cats would try to get at the foxes.

"With the frightened screams from the foxes and the yowls from the cats echoing from inside the cave and across the mountains, it pretty much sounded like a woman in distress."

A smile made its way to Dulcie's lips. "And I suppose there's an equally simple explanation for the mysterious bobbing lights?"

L. W. Rogers

Keeping his voice low, he explained that Humphrey had once worked for the railroad. "Pike said they'd tied railroad signal lanterns to long poles. As the men rode along the mountain ridges at night, the lanterns would bob about, appearing as glowing red specters. Like everything else, Humphrey was smart enough to use the notion of superstition to keep the Indians and others away from his cattle-rustling operation."

Dulcie laughed at the absurdity of his explanation. "Ingenious." Her expression grew serious. She exhaled softly. "You're going after him?"

Donovan's blue eyes darkened to almost black. "He's a heartless cur who made his wealth off the blood of innocent people. He's a man who needs killing."

"I understand," she said solemnly. "I really do." A trembling sigh shook her.

Donovan leaned forward to touch the downy fuzz on the baby's head. "When this business is over, Teaspoon will take you and the baby back to the Circle S. With Toby, Chief Three Feathers, and a few of his men, we'll push the herd to Fort Apache."

"What about you, Donovan? What will you do . . . afterward?"

He shrugged a wide shoulder, hesitant. "Once I've settled the sale, I'll send the money by Toby."

"You wouldn't consider returning to the Circle S, would you? I still need a good foreman." She worried her bottom lip with her teeth.

Unable to sit any longer, Donovan pushed to his feet. A frown knitted his brow and many thoughts plagued his mind. *You still haven't forgiven me.* "I have a ranch in Utah. It's time I go home."

A heavy silence hung between them. Donovan whirled and left as quietly as he'd entered.

* * *

Emotions played a tug-of-war between Dulcie's sensible part and her heart. Donovan had unwittingly freed her from a life of misery with a merciless man. She wondered how things would have played out if Humphrey's men hadn't recognized Donovan and called him out. Would Donovan have willingly turned the deed to the ranch over to her or claimed the Circle S as his own, ousting her and her child?

Ace Donovan . . . gambler . . . gunman . . . gentle . . . enigma.

Suddenly drained of energy, she shifted to a more comfortable position, careful not to disturb the tiny bundle cradled in her arms. She stared idly up at the ventilation hole and inhaled the lingering fragrance of crushed sage inside the tepee. A moment passed before her mood softened. Her heart disagreed with her head.

Chapter Twenty-five

Don't have no badges, but all of you riding with me, Sheriff Horn, and Donovan, raise your right hand."

Following the command, Cahill said, "I duly deputize you to uphold the law."

Chief Three Feathers, his son, and the old warriors striped their faces with war paint.

"What about me, Marshal?"

Disappointment rode Pike's face when the marshal said, "In the eyes of the law, you're still under arrest. Can't do it, son."

"If I'm gonna die, I'd rather take a bullet in a showdown than swing at the end of a rope."

"Can't fault your way of thinking." Cahill studied Pike. "All right, raise your right hand. If you come out of this alive, I'll put in a word with the federal judge."

"I won't let you down, Marshal."

Donovan worked to quell the emotions building inside him. Grasping the saddle horn, he swung into the saddle with practiced ease. As if sensing Donovan's tension, the gray snorted and pawed the earth.

"Our best chances of surprise will come after sunset." Knowing the Apache's superstitions against attacking at night, Donovan glanced at the Apache chief.

Chief Three Feathers thumped his chest. "We are deputies. We fight."

Donovan offered a nod.

170

Pike said, "Humphrey keeps a dog at the main house. It'll bark. Will attack anything that moves and responds only to Humphrey."

"Good to know, Pike," Donovan said. "Yellow Horse, you know what to do." The young Apache touched the bow and nodded his understanding.

Stars littered the sky, and the branches of piñon pine were draped in fleecy banners of mist. A chill rode on the breeze, promising an early winter.

Women and children and those too old to ride remained inside the tepees. The excited yips of village dogs broke the silence. Donovan raised his hand and signaled.

Dulcie listened to the fading cadence of departing horses. She rose from her bed and wrapped a blanket around her shoulders as she stepped from the tepee. Her eyes searched through the moonlight until she spotted the ghostly shape of the gray gelding. Its rider sat straight and tall in the saddle. She watched him vanish as if swallowed up by the silence and the dark.

She whispered, "Take care of yourself, Donovan."

The posse rode for two days, stopping long enough to rest the horses, grab a chaw of jerky, and catch a few winks.

On the third night, they slowed their horses and looked down onto the vast grasslands of the Rocking H Ranch. Smoke spiraled from the sprawling main house sitting in the middle of the distance. Light filled the windows of the bunkhouse. An occasional shadow of a man showed inside the structure.

Before allowing themselves to be skylined, Donovan used sign language to tell Yellow Horse that it was time. The young warrior slid from his pony. Settling the quiver and bow over his shoulder, he set off on silent feet.

Riders dismounted. They would wait.

Time ticked until Marshal Cahill opened the face of his

pocket watch and held it toward the moon's ray. He lifted a finger to signal one hour.

Donovan signed, "Not to worry. He'll come."

An owl's subtle deep and throaty notes mingled with the night music. Donovan answered with the mournful howling of a coyote.

Chief Three Feathers stood by Donovan's side and signed, "My son, he is here."

Like an apparition, Yellow Horse appeared. He gathered the reins of his pony and in one lithe movement swung up on the pinto's back.

Donovan knew the dog had been silenced. Without conversation, Donovan and the riders mounted up. They followed the trail to a rail fence where they tethered their horses.

Donovan motioned for the men to spread out, trusting plans would be followed. A braying laugh could be heard, making Donovan's gaze swerve toward the open door of the bunkhouse. The man's features were murky in the dim light. He instantly recognized Hank, the heavyset boozer who'd been gored while rounding up Circle S's steers. Hank laughed and slapped the back of another man who came to stand next to him on the bunkhouse porch.

Donovan reacted to Sheriff Horn's distant signal that Teaspoon and the others had surrounded the bunkhouse. He motioned for Toby, Pike, and Yellow Horse to situate themselves inside the barn door to give firepower where needed. Donovan levered the Winchester as he and Sam Cahill, in a crouch, crossed the yard. In opposite directions they stepped up on the ranch house porch and inched toward the front door.

Donovan used the rifle butt to pound against the outer wall. Weighty footsteps sounded. The heavy oak door opened. The screened door squeaked as it was swung back.

Humphrey said, "Brutus?" He called the dog's name again.

Donovan set himself squarely in front of the big man. "Been a long time, Humfried."

"Humfried?" The heavyset man's ponderous jowls deepened to a mottled red as surprise took hold. "Donovan, I thought—"

Donovan shoved the Winchester's barrel against the rotund belly. "Thought I was dead . . . just like you thought fifteen years ago when you hanged my brother and father and left me with three slugs in my chest. You were Clive Humfried then. Enforcer for the railroad."

Donovan jabbed the fat man hard.

A high-pitched voice from inside the house said, "Hey, Humphrey, what's taking so long? We've got plans to make."

Humphrey turned his snarling, jowly face away from Donovan long enough to watch Sam Cahill stride forward.

A voice across the yard yelled, "I ain't going down without a fight!"

Another voice sang out, "Me neither!"

Gunfire sounded. Someone fired an answering shot. A man screamed in pain. Sheriff Horn called, "Give it up, yardbirds! Toss out your weapons, 'cause me and my Apache posse gotcha covered."

"Looks like Tom Horn has everything under control," Marshal Cahill said as he motioned Humphrey inside the house. He glanced at Donovan. "I know that voice."

Donovan placed a finger to his lips, warning Humphrey to keep quiet. A thin man with a balding pate sat bent over a stack of papers. Without looking up, he reached for a glass. "My sources tell me another fool searching for a shortcut to Kansas is bringing his herd across the Superstition Mountains. With three thousand head tucked away in the hidden canyon, we'll rake in the profits if you keep those mangy outlaws you call drovers sober enough to make the drive."

"Obediah Stiles?" Sam Cahill's voice thundered.

Scrawny as a scratch-farm bantam, the man wearing round, wire-rimmed spectacles looked like a fish gasping for air. The glass he held slipped from his hand, spilling whiskey on the rich Persian rug.

"M-Marshall Cahill . . . w-what—" Stiles cut his eyes toward Humphrey, who stood with his hands high in the air. "I-I don't understand what's going on here."

The sudden silence rang in Donovan's ears. "Who is this man, Marshal?"

Sam Cahill glinted hard. His jaw worked in agitation. "I ought to shoot you where you stand, Stiles."

The little man covered his chest as if to protect himself. "No . . . I . . . you don't understand. It was Humphrey . . . it—"

Cahill's face tightened. "Shut up before I put my fist in your mouth.

"Donovan, meet Obediah Stiles, Indian Agent—friend and procurer of beef to the Apache, Navajo, and Havasupai."

Cahill spaced his words with forced evenness. "These people are starving, and you're reaping a profit from beef that you are authorized by the United States government to purchase and allocate to the Indians."

Stiles shrugged his bony shoulders. He dropped his hand inside his coat pocket. A smile stretched into a flat, cruel line. The first flash of fire struck Cahill below the collarbone, driving him backward.

Humphrey jabbed his elbows, catching Donovan in the chest. The lumbering fat man proved he was as resilient as rubber. Pivoting, he smashed a right in Donovan's stomach, then shoved him away and sledgehammered him with both fists in the face. The Winchester flew from Donovan's hand, the jolt rattling every bone in his body.

Donovan backed up, not liking being caught off guard. He hit Humphrey with a right to the body, then a left.

Humphrey lunged, swinging, but Donovan knocked down Humphrey's right and crossed over with his left. Humphrey gathered himself. He spat blood from his split lip. "Shoot him, Stiles. Pull the damn trigger." Humphrey's voice was thick with pain.

Donovan's body hummed with vindictive hatred. He knew exactly what kind of situation he faced. The little pip-squeak, Stiles, aimed a derringer at his forehead.

From the tail of his eye, Donovan caught the glint from the window. With no weapon other than his bow and arrows, the Apache had ruled over this vast land for generations. When the rifle was introduced they adapted to its use quickly and became expert marksmen second to none. They had fought with dignity and honor to keep their lands only to be shoved into submission by men like Humphrey and starved by men like Stiles.

In one swift, stark moment Donovan saw Yellow Horse, saw the dark-painted face, saw the arrow, and knew Stiles would meet his death.

He heard the soft whisper as the arrow zinged through the open window to find its mark, and the gasping words, "Oh God," that tore from Stiles' mouth as the arrow pierced through his jaw, tearing through his throat, and then he fell forward. With a last muscular effort he tried to roll over.

Donovan made a mad dive for the Winchester that lay across the room. Sliding on his belly, he grabbed the rifle, rolled to his back, and fired swiftly. The bullet took Humphrey under the breastbone, striking at an angle and ripping out his side. The impact knocked him against the wall. He sat up, panting and holding his side, an incredulous look on his face.

Donovan shoved to his feet. He checked on the marshal. Cahill, badly shaken, sat up. Some color had returned to his face. There was blood on his shirt. He removed the badge from his vest. "Reckon this saved me."

The derringer's bullet had struck his chest at a flat angle and, hitting the badge, had glanced away, tearing the skin beyond it with a burn rather than a wound.

The hairs on the back of Donovan's neck prickled. Instinct caused him to look up. He shoved Cahill to the floor and then sidestepped quickly as the knife sailed across the room. Donovan fired the rifle from his hip, and the bullet drove Humphrey back against the wall. His hand trembled as he lifted it to point a finger at Donovan. Death rattled in Humphrey's chest. "I know you . . . you're that sodbuster's half-blooded brat."

A lengthy silence dragged out between them. A mighty gorge of rage rose up in Donovan. He probed tersely. "Our land wasn't in the railroad's right of way. Why murder my family?"

Sucking in a laborious breath, Humphrey forced out a laugh. "Nothing personal . . . it was . . . business." His muscles convulsed and his mouth went slack as the gray mask of death covered his face.

Suddenly lost in thought, Donovan's hardened features relaxed. "The spirits of my father and brother can now rest easy."

Chapter Twenty-six

Quiet, still air, a trail bathed in moonlight, and the *clip-clop* of the gray's hooves were all that kept Donovan company as he rode toward the Circle S. The night was damp and cold, bringing a shivering chill that slid down his spine.

After delivering the cattle to Fort Apache and settling on a fair price, he'd helped Chief Three Feathers and his wranglers invest their share of the profits in a small herd. It was a new dawn for Chief Three Feathers' people, who only wanted to live in peace.

Donovan had thought about wiring a bank draft to Sheriff Horn in Blountsville and requesting that he deliver it to Dulcie, leaving him free of further obligations to her.

A ponderous sigh slipped from him as he halted the gray and stepped from the saddle. He untied the sheepskin coat draped across the back of his saddle and pulled the coat up over his shoulders.

A month of hard cold days and nights in the saddle brought him to the wooded slope above Mossy Creek.

He'd had hours of silence, hours to think, hours to reason why he was returning to the Circle S when he should have ridden in the opposite direction to his ranch in Utah. No matter how much his mind and heart warred against each other, his reasoning came full circle. He was returning to Dulcie. Would she have him?

He found a thick copse of trees in which to bed down. He swung out of the saddle and secured his mount. He was weary from long hours of traveling and stretched to ease the ache in his back.

Away for two months, one more night under the stars wouldn't matter.

Dulcie woke to an unearthly brilliance seeping through the partly shuttered window. She shivered; the room was as cold as the ashes in the hearth. The temperature had dropped with the arrival of a cold front, catching Mossy Creek in its glory of golden fall foliage.

She crept from her bed. Wrapped in a blanket, she crossed to the window, tracking the brilliance to its source. The moon shone down on a world dressed in a mantle of white flocking. The trees, the buildings of the Circle S, the very earth itself as far as the eye could see was cloaked in not ice or rain, yet not quite snow.

A wail distracted Dulcie. She padded to the cradle and lifted the baby into her arms and held her to the window. "Look, Maggie. It's so beautiful, like a fairyland."

The child yawned and whimpered. Dulcie smiled as she drew the shutter completely shut. "You're wet and cold as a frog, my little daughter." After changing the baby's wet clothing and wrapping her in a quilt, Dulcie settled the baby inside the cradle Teaspoon had built.

She walked barefoot across the cold floor to gather kindling from the woodbox. After stoking new life into the embers, she went to peer out the window. Nothing moved, nothing stirred.

A chill tickled the hair on her arms. She wanted to be angry with Donovan. She wanted to blame him for all her troubles. She wanted to call him names, tell him he was a heartless cur who thought only of himself. She turned from the window, knowing Donovan wasn't the source of her problems. As things went, she was grateful for the two old Apache who'd come to help Teaspoon and to learn ranching.

A trembling sigh shook her. *Two months. It's been two months.* Thoughts plagued her. Had Donovan sold the herd? Had he taken her money and gambled it away? After all, he was a gambler, wasn't he?

"Where are you, Donovan?" Her voice broke the quiet.

She knew to the penny how much money was inside the crock cookie jar. All wasn't lost. She would sell off a few head of cows to pay the taxes and to buy supplies. No, all was not lost.

Drawing the curtain against the brightness of the winter moon, Dulcie climbed back into bed. A half smile lifted the corner of her mouth. *I'll give Donovan two more days, then I'll drive into Blountstown and put the ranch up for sale.*

Satisfied with her plan, she snuggled deep in the quilt's warmth and closed her eyes.

The morning sky was bathed in spectacular hues of magenta and dulled to a dark grayish-blue on the western horizon. Puffy white clouds seemed to glow as they drifted near the sun's face.

Donovan relished the zesty tingle as the crisp morning air caressed his bare chest and washed the last dregs of sleep from his eyes. He stretched his right arm upward, then winced slightly as the muscles twitched in his back, a frequent and painful reminder of his most recent wounds.

A chilly breeze wafted over him, eliciting a shiver and prompting him to pull a woolen shirt over his shoulders and tuck the tails inside his chinos.

The gray gelding greeted Donovan with soft whickers. The horse pawed at the dusting of snow.

Donovan spoke to the animal as he smoothed the blanket across its broad back before setting the saddle in place. "I hear you, General. If things play out right, we'll both have a full belly and a warm shelter over our heads tonight."

Donovan fastened the cinch and lowered the stirrup in place. His gaze drifted toward the spiral of smoke rising from the ranch house chimney. He tugged on the heavy jacket and hauled into the saddle.

Dulcie cracked eggs into the iron skillet, and while the egg whites curled brown at the edges, she burned her fingers hauling another pan filled with biscuits out of the oven. She carried the hot, fluffy bread to the table and dumped them on a platter, then turned back to the stove to salvage the frying eggs. She glanced with a smile at the blissful gurgles from the baby whose cradle sat in front of the fireplace.

A chill had crept down off the mountains and stolen through the valley in subtle foreshadowings of the winter to come. The door banged back against the wall, and Dulcie gasped and then spun to look, only to find the door had been victim to the gusting breeze. She walked over and closed the door and started to secure the bolt, but she paused in the middle of her effort as she glimpsed a movement in the morning light. She tensed as she spied the gray gelding crossing the creek toward the house.

Teaspoon bounded up the porch steps. He lifted a fist to pound on the door when Dulcie opened it wide. "It's him, Miz Dulcie. Donovan . . . he's here."

Donovan sat hunched in the saddle, the collar of the sheepskin coat pulled high on his neck.

She stepped to the porch, pulling the door shut behind her. She crossed her arms over her chest and tapped her foot. Flooded with emotions, anger scorched her as deeply as the burn on her fingers. She harrumphed. "It's about time."

"Now, Miz Dulcie, that ain't no way for you to go feelin'. He came back, didn't he? Didn't have to . . . could've just sent the money to Sheriff Horn and rode on to Utah without so much as a fare-thee-well."

"Oh, all right. He probably hasn't had a decent meal in weeks." Her heart thumped against the wall of her chest. Although she felt like a scatterbrained girl at her first dance, she told herself it was from pure anger. "Tell Buffalo Who Runs and Spotted Owl to wash up. Breakfast is ready."

Teaspoon flashed an impatient frown. "You mean you ain't gonna have a private meal with Donovan?" He shook his head in disbelief. "You keep on and you'll choke to death on all that vengeance you've been harboring these many weeks. If you ask my opinion—"

"What I think is that you should mind your own business, Mr. Teaspoon Griffin."

"Donovan is a good man. He took care of all of us on the trail . . . lest you forgot, Miz Dulcie." Teaspoon slapped a gloved hand against the side of his pants. "And dagnabit, I ain't moving off this porch till I give him a proper howdy."

Gritting her teeth and steeling herself against the frigid air, she watched the gelding cross the yard like a fabled gray ghost. "Oh, all right, Teaspoon. You remind me of a nagging fishwife." Her heartbeat was far from steady as she lifted her face to catch a stingy ray of sun.

It infuriated her that Donovan acted as if nothing had passed between them as he halted the gray gelding at the edge of the steps. His blue eyes flashed and his lethal grin broadened before he tried to look serious again.

He tipped his hat. "Dulcie . . . Teaspoon."

"Unless your hide's permanently attached to the saddle, step down and light a spell. Miz Dulcie's fixed a fine breakfast, and I was 'bout to call the hands in." Teaspoon reached up to pump Donovan's gloved hand up and down.

"Hands?"

"Yup. Buffalo Who Runs and Spotted Owl. You 'member them?"

Dulcie momentarily lifted her gaze. "You may as well step down. Breakfast is getting cold."

Donovan slid from the saddle and tossed the reins over the hitching post and then descended the wooden steps.

Dulcie smoothed the skirt of her calico dress. "It was admirable of you to help Chief Three Feathers invest in a herd. He wanted Yellow Horse to learn ranching, but when the boy expressed more interest in raising horses than cows, Toby's father said he needed another young man to help out. Buffalo Who Runs and Spotted Owl work here for board and found until they are ready to return to the village."

As if her dissertation was enough, she pressed her lips together, pivoted on her heel, and entered the house.

Donovan seemed to read Dulcie's thoughts and a sad smile rested on his mouth and settled around his eyes. She would not allow him to forget that he'd hired on under false pretenses and had never mentioned the deed to the ranch. From the corner of his eye he watched as she busied herself pouring another round of coffee.

"How'd things go with Pike in Fort Apache?" Teaspoon grabbed another biscuit and slathered it with butter.

"True to his word, Sam Cahill spoke on Pike's behalf to the judge. He explained how Pike had volunteered to help capture Humphrey's outlaw band and how his knowledge of the ranch layout and the dog had been instrumental in swift justice with a minimal loss of lives. Cahill even said Pike would make a fine deputy."

"Yeah, what'd the judge say to that?"

Donovan could have smiled, but he didn't. "The judge took Sam at his word and remanded Pike into his custody for a period of five years. Sam pinned a badge on Pike the same day."

"Well, if I ain't a hornswaggled toad. Pike a deputy."

Silence fell around the room until the two Apache pushed back their chairs. "Ho, Donovan, we have much work." Spotted Owl lifted a hand before he and Buffalo Who Runs left the house.

Donovan reached beneath his shirt and pulled out an envelope. He laid it in front of Dulcie's plate. "Even after settling wages with Toby and the chief, you made a tidy profit. It's all there . . . including Teaspoon's share."

He wanted to touch her cheek, her hand, her shoulder. He didn't dare. Instead, he shoved from the chair and lifted the baby from the cradle.

"Maggie has grown some since I last saw her."

The baby cooed and reached up her tiny hands.

Teaspoon slugged down the last of his coffee. "Think I'll take myself outside. 'Pears you and Miz Dulcie have some unsettled business."

When the front door closed, Dulcie blinked and thrust her chin. "I'm not sure I can forgive you, Donovan." She wet her lips and wondered why she wanted to cover her face and weep inconsolably.

"Sheriff Horn and a judge cleared me of killing Jack Slaughter."

"It's more than that. You deceived me . . . kept your name a secret . . . why didn't you just own up to who you were, that you'd killed my husband and given me the deed to the ranch? I don't know that I can ever trust you."

He couldn't refute any of her charges. "If I could take it all back, I would. Fact is I can't. What's done is done."

His eyes, their blue depths revealing a mixture of anger and remorse, glanced down at the baby who'd grown fretful. He held the child out to her mother.

Cradling the baby in her arms, Dulcie stood quietly staring into the flickering fireplace. Her shoulders lifted as she sighed.

Donovan took a moment to rub the tired muscles in his neck before he moved to the door. His brows knitted together.

"Dulcie, look at me."

The baby cuddled against her shoulder, Dulcie complied and silently watched his tall, proud frame.

"There's a bond between us. We both knew it from that first day I rode into the yard. I can't undo who I am or the things I've done." He waited for her to digest that.

He reached out to touch her cheek, and when she flinched he drew his hand away. "You can't have a future, Dulcie, until you let go of the past. Start a new future for you and the baby with me . . . in Utah."

When she didn't respond, he grabbed his hat from the peg and slapped it on his head.

Without knowing that Teaspoon stood outside the door eavesdropping, Donovan opened it with such force that the old wrangler toppled backward.

"You ain't ridin' out, are you?"

"Man can't stay where he isn't wanted." Donovan didn't bother setting his toe in the stirrup. He grabbed the saddle horn, and swinging into the saddle, wheeled the gray toward the creek.

The baby still in her arms, Dulcie hesitated, then walked to the porch. She swallowed hard and blinked back the tears.

"Dagnabit, girl, you're a danged fool if you let a good man like Donovan ride out of your life," Teaspoon said.

A stinging shame whipped through her heart. Her slim shoulders drooped. "It's too late." She watched Donovan's broad back and listened to the faint footfalls of the gelding as they rode toward the creek.

"If you don't go after him, it'll be the most regretful mistake you'll ever make for the rest of your life." Teaspoon took the baby from her arms. "Git on now. Once he crosses the creek you'll never catch him."

The thought made a lonely ache in her heart. She felt torn in two, but in the end she knew no matter what had happened before, she wanted to be his. It was time to forgive the differences. She'd tried hard to suppress her affection for Donovan. Yet, over the months of waiting, her feelings for him had grown into a deep, abiding love.

"What if it's too late, Teaspoon? What if he won't have me?"

"Ye'll never know if you stand there askin' foolish questions. Dagnabit, girl, light a fire under your feet."

Without hesitation, she placed a quick peck on the old man's cheek, lifted her skirt, and fled down the steps.

"Donovan . . . Donovan!" Her voice rose louder as her feet seemed to sprout wings, carrying her toward the creek.

Hearing his name, he turned in the saddle to see Dulcie, her skirt lifted high and her feet pumping. The hair that reminded him of summer wheat had come loose from its pins and fluttered in the breeze.

He turned the gray and gigged him into a lope, halting in front of the panting woman.

She straightened her spine a little, then smiled a small wobbly smile. The words blurted out before she could call them back. "Marry me, Donovan."

He hadn't expected that. She could have said almost anything and he would have been fine, but he hadn't expected a marriage proposal.

She saw the puzzlement in his expression as he stared down at her. She swallowed the lump in her throat. Maybe she'd waited too long. Maybe he'd reject her. Not that she'd blame him.

And then he smiled. "Tell me why I should marry you, Dulcie."

"Maggie needs a father . . . I need you too."

"Not a good enough reason." He wheeled the gelding.

"Wait." She bit down on her bottom lip and swallowed all her fears. "You don't have to love me, Donovan, but I love you."

He held her gaze. "Be sure, Dulcie."

"I'm more certain than I've ever been about anything in my whole life."

There was nothing he could say to that. He reached down and lifted her across his lap, wrapping her in his arms. "Shall we go home?"

"Only if it's to Utah." She lifted her gaze to stare up at him.

A great tension seemed to leave Donovan, and his serious expression melted into a smile. "I suppose we have to take Teaspoon with us."

Dulcie blushed a little as she laughed. "He'll be the only grandpa Maggie will ever know."

"Then I reckon we'd better go tell him the news." Donovan nudged the gray into a shuffling walk toward the old wrangler standing on the porch with the baby cradled in his arms.

Dulcie placed her head against Donovan's broad chest. She listened to the steady beating of his heart. Feelings of excitement, joy, and anticipation rushed through her.

"Tell me about your ranch."

Donovan wrapped his strong arms around her, hugging her close. "It has green meadows where long-legged foals frisk alongside their mothers, where shadows gather in darkness under the trees, quiet shadows. It's home, and I've been away too long."

He would build a new house, and the woman beside him would be there, with a sleeping child in her arms.

Never had he experienced such harmony between his heart and his head.